Friends for Keeps

Heartlines

Books by Pam Lyons

A Boy Called Simon
He Was Bad
It Could Never Be
Latchkey Girl
Danny's Girl
Odd Girl Out
Ms Perfect

Books by Anita Eires

Tug Of Love
Summer Awakening
Spanish Exchange
Star Dreamer
Californian Summer
If Only . . .
Teacher's Pet
Working Girl

Books by Mary Hooper

Love Emma XXX
Follow That Dream
My Cousin Angie
Happy Ever After
Opposites Attract
A Love Like Yours

Books by Barbara Jacobs

Two Times Two

Books by Jane Pitt

Loretta Rose
Autumn Always Comes
Stony Limits
Rainbows For Sale
Pia
The Boy Who Was Magic

Books by Ann de Gale

Island Encounter
Hands Off!

Books by Anthea Cohen

Dangerous Love

Books by David S Williams

Give Me Back My Pride
Forgive and Forget

Books by Jill Young

Change Of Heart
Three Summers On

Books by Ann Ruffell

Friends For Keeps
Secret Passion
Baby Face

Books by Lorna Read

Images
The Name Is Zero

Books by Jane Butterworth

Spotlight On Sam

Books by John Harvey

Wild Love
Last Summer, First Love

Books by Anita Davies

Stepsisters

Heartlines

Ann Ruffell

Friends for Keeps

A Pan Original

First published 1985 by Pan Books Ltd,
Cavaye Place, London SW10 9PG
9 8 7 6 5 4 3 2
© Ann Ruffell 1985
ISBN 0 330 28639 0
Phototypeset by Input Typesetting Ltd, London
Printed and bound in Great Britain by
Hunt Barnard Printing, Aylesbury, Bucks

Chapter 1

My mother is so embarrassing.

Alan — he's my best friend — he says, well at least you can talk to her. Talk to her! You should try not talking to her! I mean, that's another of the embarrassing things. No, that's not quite true. She doesn't mind if you say nothing, but she'll be all understanding about it so that by the end of your period of silence you wish you'd said something after all.

Sonia — my best friend at school — says I'm lucky, at least my mother will talk about all the things she'd like to talk to *her* mother about. But I wish she didn't. You see, she'll wheedle things out of you — things you'd rather she didn't know — like the time I went on the back of John's motorbike when he was still on a provisional licence. My mother actually asked where I'd been, and before I knew what I was doing I'd told her. Of course, she then went on and told everyone else and it was right round town in five minutes flat. It was lucky nobody told the police, I suppose, though it couldn't have been much worse.

Sonia's mum, well, she just screamed the place down and said Sonia wasn't to come round to our house any more or even be friends with me, even though Sonia didn't have anything to do with it at all.

She forgot about it after a week. She always does. But the thing was, as Sonia said, even if she swore blind she had nothing to do with it her mother wouldn't listen.

Of course, my mother didn't go on like Sonia's mum. She said, 'Now let's have a little chat.' My stomach always curls up when she says this. It means you get put in a chair, like a sort of interrogation, with Dad looking on and putting his oar in at times, and she goes on all about the rights and wrongs and what did I think about it and couldn't I have talked gently to John and reminded him what a risk he was taking? She makes you answer, my mother. That's what I mean about you try *not* to talk to her.

But I'd better tell you about Alan first, in case you get the wrong idea. He's taller than me, quite slim, nice brown hair and eyes. Just ordinary looking. We've been friends since we were in the cradle. Literally. Our mums used to live next door to each other and they'd say googly things to us in our prams, cooing when we were trying to gouge each other's eyes out, saying, 'Wouldn't it be nice if . . .' and then, 'Won't it be nice when . . .' At least, that's what Alan says his mother said. I don't really know because I hardly ever see her now. We don't live next door any more and Alan comes over to us more than I go there.

I suppose it isn't really surprising that they've always thought of us as boy and girl friend. We used to go around together at school until after his O levels when Alan decided he wasn't going to stay on at school any longer and went to college to do his A's. I've got to do my O levels this year. As for me leaving and not going into the sixth form — if I get any O levels, that is — there'd be such a business with my parents being understanding and wanting to know all the reasons that I don't really think it would be worth it. Alan laughs at me when I threaten to run away. He says he'd have stayed at school if they'd let him grow a beard, and he knows my mother would let me leave if I wanted to. (I've never quite understood why he hasn't grown a beard after all.)

You see he's known my mother for years and years and sort of got used to her from an early age so he doesn't get quite as put off as everyone else. It's nice that I've got at least one friend I can ask round without having to apologise, even if it does mean my mother goes all secret-smiles and dewey-eyed when he's around and she thinks I'm not looking. And she always brightens up when he's here because she can discuss things like whether I really ought to have my hair dyed since it's against the school rules and of course if it wasn't too obvious she doesn't see why I shouldn't because it doesn't make me more badly behaved or less willing to work . . .

You see — you can't even go *against* my mother. She's always got a good reason for both sides. It makes me wild, because Alan will argue with her and then she'll change tack and say he's quite right, so he goes and argues on the side my mother was on in the first place.

'She just likes a good argument,' Alan said when I went on at him about this.

'I don't,' I told him. 'I just wish I knew what she really thinks.'

'What for?' said Alan. 'She doesn't stop you from

7

doing anything, does she?'

This is another problem. I wish she did. I mean, all my friends' parents say, 'You mustn't go out with this boy,' or 'No, you can't have a party,' or, if they say you can have a party, they insist on being there. If I wanted a party, first of all my parents would have a long discussion about it, then they'd say yes, of course, and they'd go out and leave you to it, just like that.

You must be wondering why I'm complaining. It sounds just perfect. But it isn't. They don't *just* say yes. You have to justify it. I mean, she makes you think, and I don't think at the moment I want to think, much.

If I take my other friends home she'll start talking to them as well and asking them what they think. It's not just about dyed hair and parties. I wouldn't mind so much if it was just that. But she talks to you about sex and babies until it just makes me want to curl up. My friends do talk to her when they come round, but afterwards . . .

'Isn't your mother a scream, Frankie?' they'll say. 'Does she really mean all those things she says?'

I don't really know whether she means them or not. I've an idea that sometimes she only says things because she thinks this is the progressive way to go on. One thing I *do* know, though. I'd never take a boyfriend home. I mean, if she started on them like that! I bet she'd ask him whether he wanted to sleep with me and then start discussing whether he should or he shouldn't. My face gets red enough when my ordinary friends are there. A boyfriend – no. I wouldn't take him home at all.

Now I've let it out.

I met him in the college common room one evening when Alan was playing a squash match or something equally athletic and boring. It's funny how I stay being friends with Alan because some of the things he does are so crazy, like playing games and going to look at art galleries.

Anyway, I was waiting with Sonia and a couple of other girls from our form, when *he* came in.

My heart went bump. Just like that.

I've never felt anything like that before, and all I'd done was look at him from a distance. He walked over to the coffee machine, and I just couldn't take my eyes away.

'Frankie, what are you staring at?'

'Who's that?' I hissed, my eyes still on him.

'Who?' It was one of the others, Caroline, I think.

'Over there. By the coffee machine.'

'Oh, him. That's Clive.'

Clive. The name suited him so well, somehow. I didn't even listen to the rest of what Caroline was saying. I think she was telling me whose brother he was or something, but I just couldn't stop looking. He was really fantastic looking: dark hair, and deep blue eyes set in a sort of natural shadow that a girl would give her right arm for.

'You all right, Frankie?' It was Sonia this time. 'What are you staring at?'

'Clive.' It was such a dreamy sort of name. I wanted to roll it round my teeth.

'Oh, him.'

He was still at the coffee machine. Sometimes the thing goes wrong and you have to hit it before anything happens. He was kicking at the front of it, trying to get it to work. The way I was watching, it was as if he was in the final of some Olympic strong-man competition, and so for a while I didn't cotton on to Sonia's tone or the way she was looking.

I turned back, sighing, and caught her dirty look. Then I remembered. I'd never seen him before, she wouldn't ever let me meet him, and if I hadn't been so enchanted with the name attached to that person over there, I'd have latched on a bit quicker.

And then he came over, paper cup of coffee in hand, and you could feel Sonia literally freezing. She unfroze enough to say, stiffly, as if her mouth was full of icicles, 'Oh, Clive, this is my friend, Frances,' and give me a murderous look. I knew what it meant. I was to make some excuse to go, and go. So I didn't.

'Hi,' I said.

'Hi,' said Clive, and sat down between us. Sonia moved so fast you'd have thought he was sending out an electrical charge – which he was, to me, but not in that way. She stayed on the bench, but she couldn't have got much further away from him. I knew when Clive sat down between us that whatever he'd seen in Sonia before, he didn't see now. Sonia's mum's cakes and puds, though my mouth still waters at the thought of them, have not been kind to Sonia. She is frankly overweight, and a new spot was erupting to join the others on her chin. That is one thing about my mum and her health foods. You don't get nearly as many spots, though I'd never let her think she was right.

Sonia had gone out with Clive for a couple of months. It was all very secretive. It was the first time

Sonia had kept anything from me and I was naturally upset at the time. When your best girlfriend suddenly says she won't come to the disco this week, won't come with the gang to so and so's party, won't come shopping in town, then you begin to wonder if she likes you any more. I missed her most when I had a bit of money to spend. Alan likes clothes, but you can hardly trail a boy into the communal changing rooms at Miss Selfridge.

I still don't know how she managed to keep him away from everyone. I mean, my best friend, and I never even knew what he looked like.

But that was a year ago. And I hadn't heard anyone mention him since.

Until now.

Perhaps I began to understand Sonia. It was the first thing I would do, keep him away from any other female. And here he was, sitting next to me in the dingy coffee bar, surrounded by paper cups and tattered notices, when you felt he ought to be leaning nonchalantly against a pillar in some exotic place.

We just talked, that time. Sonia got up and went, quite soon, but Caroline and Jane stayed until Alan came back, in a vile mood because he'd lost, and we all went off into town afterwards. Without Sonia. I didn't mind at all, in a bitchy sort of way. It served her right for leaving me for two months a year ago.

And then I started scheming how I could see him again, get him to ask me out. Was he going to Caroline's party next week? Did he ever go to the skating rink? There was no point hoping to bump into him again in the college: I was at school all week and only came here this evening because of Alan's match, and even then I wouldn't if we hadn't all been going out straight afterwards.

My mother would have said, 'Why don't you ask him? It's only an ordinary friendly question.'

But it wasn't. I wanted him so much I couldn't, I just couldn't. I just let him say goodbye to us all in the crowd, and disappear, and then, of course, it was too late.

Chapter 2

I used to think when people went on about the sky shining more brightly or the world seeming greener when you were in love, it was all a load of rubbish. I was wrong.

When I remembered that dingy common room, always half empty in the early evening when we waited for Alan to smuggle us in to the adult films, it seemed the most desirable place on earth. That wonderful machine, with its bad-tempered habit of refusing to hand out the coffee or chocolate or tea, was a streamlined, 'Doctor Who' invention. Even its foibles had some point. It had made Clive stand there for ten minutes. If he had got his coffee instantly he might have strolled away, and I'd never have met him. The dirty cream walls and scratched benches had a romantic, historic character in my eyes now. He had sat on that plastic cushioning. The stained formica-topped table had the mark of his paper cup on it.

And yet I'd never felt so miserable in all my life. I tried to tell myself I was being stupid. I was. But it didn't make any difference. I still went around at school, at home, down the street, in town, in a haze of alternate black misery and dreamy longing. If I was praised for a good essay, got a reasonable mark in maths, I was filled with undying gratitude. My happiness was as if *he* had said these nice things, shown his appreciation. And if my hair went wrong – which it always did, every morning – or I got shouted at for some ridiculous thing by teachers or my parents, I felt like crying. Not because they were criticising, or because my hair was awful, but because I always thought of it being him who was criticising, or saying my hair was awful.

Then I'd have to cheer myself up by thinking, 'He wouldn't criticise. He'd always say marvellous things to me.'

I'd dream about them, every night.

I asked Alan if he knew him. I just wanted to know any tiny detail, it didn't matter what. I'd be satisfied with information about when his first teeth came through, what his favourite colour was, even how many girlfriends he had had. Though I didn't really want to know about them. The trouble was, Alan was very cagey about him. I didn't want to ask too much in case he realised why I was interested. I suppose it showed, eventually.

'Clive? Oh, yes, I see him from time to time.' This was his reply to my first question. Not very helpful. I probed a bit further.

13

'What course is he doing?' I said, I thought, lightly.

'How should I know?' I'd never heard Alan being *cross* before. Angry, yes, or furious about some world-wide injustice. Not cross. It seemed almost pettish. I didn't understand it at all.

'Sorry I spoke,' I said peevishly. He growled something and walked off rather fast, not waiting for any of us. He didn't come round that evening. He doesn't always, and I don't really expect him, but that time it seemed to mean something.

But I did start getting upset when he was almost rude every single time I mentioned Clive's name. And as if to punish me for mentioning him, he didn't turn up for a whole week. My mother made a few comments, but I said something about his having a lot of studying to do, which could have been true. I almost believed it myself. And when he did come round, walking in as if he owned the place, it was as much as I could do not to shout, 'And where do you think you've been?' Silly, really, because he's often not come round for days. It was just that I wanted to know about Clive so much, and he was the only person who could tell me. Just as well he was in a good mood again because I couldn't keep it in any longer. What could I do to make him notice me? How could I get to know him? Where was he likely to be? What sort of things did he like?

Alan looked at me critically.

'All right, you've known me long enough. I'd have thought you knew what I looked like by now,' I said sharply.

'I don't,' he said, as if surprised.

'What do you mean?'

'I mean I've known you for so long it hadn't occurred to me to look at you.'

'All right, stop being clever.' I was getting a bit fed up with this. He was beginning to sound like my mother. She'd just gone off, fussing about making us some nice wholemeal sandwiches for supper.

'I'm not being clever,' said Alan mildly. 'I'm trying to look at you from a potential boyfriend point of view.'

This would be, of course, the point when my mother chose to come in with the sandwiches. Her eyes glistened a bit and you could see she was trying hard not to say anything. It didn't work very well.

'Oh, Alan!' she said.

'Purely academic,' I snarled, and stamped out to my own room upstairs. At least they wouldn't follow me there. It was in a filthy mess, as usual, and I felt annoyed at it. Why couldn't she be like other mothers and come in and tidy it up once in a while? Or even make me tidy it? You do need someone to nag at you sometimes. It's only Sonia that ever turns up her nose and says what a disgusting hole it is, and that's even more irritating. I mean, it isn't for her to say. At least my mother doesn't come and snoop around. I can leave the most private things lying about and be quite sure nobody will look at them.

Just as well. There were lots of bits of paper with Clive's name on all over the place. It gave me a nice feeling, just writing his name down and knowing that nobody knew about it. I wrote lots of other boys' names down as well, just in case. Sonia has a nasty habit of snooping round when she's here and we go to my room for a gossip. I didn't want her sharp eyes looking too hard at something I'd left around by accident.

They ate all the sandwiches, and never thought of bringing me one. Dad got the last, just before I came down, when he came in late from a meeting.

It looked as if Alan was out, as far as getting to know Clive better was concerned.

And I kept going to that awful college every night, just on the off chance of seeing him, and he never seemed to be there. It wasn't surprising, I suppose. I knew he ought to be holding up an Adam fireplace, not fighting with a temperamental coffee machine. He'd probably gone back to the Greek Islands, or Park Lane, or wherever it was he belonged. He certainly wouldn't be interested in a person like me.

On the other hand, he had been interested in Sonia, even if it was only for a short time. How had she managed it? And last year, when she'd only have been just fifteen.

I asked her in break at school, when we'd been herded outside in spite of the weather. I can see why Alan left. It really would be nice to be treated like an adult and not have to be pushed out in the pouring rain because it's good for our characters.

She was very cagey about it, even though nobody, not even Caroline, was anywhere near us.

'I don't know,' she said.

'Of course you know,' I said, feeling niggled. 'Did you ask him, or did he ask you? And how?'

'Oh – it was ages ago.'

Sometimes I really wonder about my friends. But she wouldn't budge, and every time I tried to say anything about Clive she'd walk off and talk to someone else, or pretend she was terribly interested in getting her homework done in advance – something Sonia *never* does.

And all this made me wonder even more about him. And feel even more crazy about him. And then – it was almost like a re-run of the last time – Caz, Jane, Sonia and I were all hanging about waiting for Alan to finish another of his interminable matches – there *he* was, fighting with the coffee machine again.

He looked over with that devastating smile, and I *swear* it was directed straight at me.

My heart missed a beat. I nearly panicked. I just wanted to run away, out of the college altogether. I was just about to when he came over.

I could feel my smile, too wide, showing too many teeth.

'Hello Clive,' I said brightly. 'Where have you been all this time?'

I could feel Sonia's eyes, murderous, on me.

'Oh, out and about,' he said noncommittally. 'How are you all?'

He settled himself down comfortably between Caz and Jane. Disappointment rose like sickness, and I had to swallow hard. He hadn't been smiling particularly at me after all.

'Isn't it terrible coffee?' I heard myself say, too loudly. 'Actually, if you want anything that tastes of itself, instead of whatever the person before you has had, you ought to try the hot chocolate.'

'I have,' he smiled, holding up the plastic cup. 'But it tastes of tea.'

They all laughed, but I'm sure I laughed loudest.

I don't remember any more of that evening. Just

as well. I know I must have made an awful fool of myself. I was the first one to go home. I didn't even wait for Alan. And I'm sure I heard the other girls sniggering when I went through the glass doors – you know the way you're terribly conscious of your body, and your bottom wriggles without you wanting it to, and when you try to stop it your legs go so stiff you can hardly put one in front of the other. I wanted badly to turn round and give a friendly wave as I went but my neck seemed to have seized up.

Perhaps it wasn't as bad as all that. At school next day nobody said anything, and if I'd really looked a fool Sonia would have told me, especially in the bitchy state of mind she was in just now. But I knew Clive had noticed. He couldn't not have noticed. He must have been really amused.

Well, that was that, I thought. He'll never be interested in me now. I tried not to think about him, but now my hands doodled his name all over my history book at school as if I didn't have anything to do with them. It was going to be on there a long time, too, because I'd only just started the book and it would take me all the rest of term to fill it up and get a new one. I suppose I could always have 'lost' it, but then I found I was writing *Clive* all over my other books.

I kept away from the college. We only went because it was somewhere to meet that was warm and cheap. My friends' parents don't really like their houses filled with teenagers and besides they always have really boring television programmes on all the time. And at the college you can go swimming or play squash or badminton or table tennis really cheaply. Alan can do all these things for nothing, because he's a student there, so we often make him pay for the coffee. Anyway, it was time I did some studying with O levels coming up. My mother was beginning to compose lectures about how as far as she was concerned it didn't really matter if I wanted to go on to higher education or not, but the more I could do, the more choice I'd have later on, and all that sort of thing.

Oh, I know she was right, but I wasn't in the mood for it. I wish she'd just say, 'Frankie, you've got to stay in and do at least two hours' work each night,' like Sonia's mother does. But to make you do the thinking, and feel guilty about it . . .

Anyway, Sonia's mum did start clamping down and there wasn't anyone to go around with. Caz and Jane were really friends together, and without Sonia I didn't feel like butting in. Then they stopped going swimming for some reason and I hadn't got an excuse, except for going to swim or play table tennis or go to a film with Alan, but somehow he seemed to have gone funny since I asked him about Clive. I suppose he doesn't like him, but it's very strange that he hasn't said so. Normally Alan is so straight with me about anything. He likes arguing, sure, but if you want the truth about anything he'll give it to you.

But then I never asked what he thought about Clive. Only what he thought Clive might think about me. And he was a bit cagey about that too. I suppose I didn't want to ask his opinion about Clive in case he hadn't got a good one. I didn't really care if he was bad, or even if he'd been in prison or borstal or anything like that. If there was anything wrong about him I knew I'd be able to reform him, and I didn't

19

want anyone else telling me about it; I'd find out for myself.

'Are you all right, Frankie?'

My mother was looking at me with that sympathetic concerned face of hers which she puts on when she's anxious about me. It was 'talking time'.

'Yes,' I said stiffly, hoping she couldn't read my thoughts. I was going to find it difficult enough keeping my attraction for Clive away from her, let alone my lurid fantasies about him.

'You look as if you need to talk to someone,' pursued my mother, sitting down beside me on the settee. 'You know you can say anything to me, don't you? No need to be afraid. Is it something about sex you don't understand? Or perhaps some boyfriend trouble? I noticed that you and Alan weren't . . .'

'It's nothing to do with anything like that,' I said sharply and got up from the settee as if a fuse had been lit under me. 'Why do you always think everything's got something to do with sex?'

'Or school work?' she went on, unperturbed, just as if I hadn't screamed at her. 'We're always willing to try to help, you know, if we can. I'm a bit blurry about maths, as you know, but anything else . . .'

'No, it's nothing to do with school work,' I said, though I knew if I didn't stop daydreaming it very soon would be. 'In fact, there's nothing wrong at all. I wish you'd stop going on at me.'

It was very brave of me. I think that was the first time I'd ever stood up to her like that.

'Well, you know we're always here if you want to talk,' she said, and drifted off to the kitchen to think about creating something cordon bleu for tomorrow.

I don't know why she bothers to do that either. Everything's ruined because she insists on using wholemeal flour, and all the things that ought to come out mouth-wateringly fluffy are as heavy as bricks.

Frankie, you're a spoiled brat, I told myself silently. Stop behaving like a two-year-old.

My talking-to to myself didn't work. I went on behaving like a spoiled brat, only now I felt guilty about it.

If only, I thought, Clive would ask me out I'd be happy as a king.

I seemed to hear the voices of both Alan and my mother saying, 'What makes you think kings are happy?' and I hated them both because that was the sort of thing they *would* say, taking all the fun out of things.

And the last thing I could ask, and the only thing I wanted to ask, was 'How do I get him to like me enough to ask me out?'

But I was still ashamed of that prattling me that had monopolised the conversation and sparkled like cheap tinsel, and even when Alan, rather abruptly, came by one evening and said he was going swimming would I like to come, I made some lame excuse about having too much homework and no money anyway.

'As you like,' said Alan equably, and went away.

I cried in my bed that night. It was a Thursday again. He might have been there. There wouldn't have been anyone else to show off in front of. I should have gone.

But it was another week before Alan breezed in

again and said, 'There's a good film on tonight at the college. Want to come? I'll pay.'

'You don't have to,' I said. 'What is it?'

It was a film I'd wanted to see yonks ago but had missed. You can't always rely on them turning up on television later on, and we don't have a video. So in spite of the fact that college films were liable to break down in the middle and you had to put up with people's heads getting in the way in front of you, I said yes.

'No homework?' said Alan wickedly as we left the house.

'Plenty,' I said, 'but I think I've done enough home-work these last few weeks to deserve a night of two-sentence essays done before breakfast.'

I was full of flippant remarks that evening, especially as the film wasn't as good as I'd thought it was going to be, there was a very tall bloke with fuzzy hair right in front who kept wriggling his head from side to side, and Clive was nowhere to be seen.

I hadn't really expected him, of course, but there had always been that slim chance that he might be fighting with the coffee machine again, and I didn't really believe it when he was.

I was too shocked to be flippant or show-offish. I didn't even say sharply that I thought he ought to have got the measure of the coffee machine by now. I simply sat there looking, he said afterwards, like a frightened bird.

'Frankie.' No, not even with a question mark. He knew who I was. I felt a warm, bubbling feeling rise up from my stomach. I dared to smile.

'Hello, Clive.'

22

I don't know whether I managed to make it sound natural. It didn't sound at all natural to me, but Alan said, 'Oh, hello Clive,' as well and got up before I could really analyse it. I began to panic. I didn't want to go, not now, please not just now.

'I'm just going to the library to see if that book's still there,' he said. 'Do you want me to see you home or are you all right?'

'Oh – I'm all right – thanks,' I said. I didn't look at him, only at Clive.

I didn't even see him go, because Clive sat down right beside me with this terrible cup of coffee – or was it chocolate? – in his hands and said, 'I don't really know why I got this. You were right about it – it doesn't taste of what it says on the button you push. I'm still trying to work out if it's because the buttons are in the wrong place or someone filled up the powder backwards.'

I laughed. It didn't sound natural, a bit wobbly, but better than last time – last time? He'd *listened*, he remembered, even if I had babbled.

'In fact,' he continued, 'I think I could bear to leave it behind. I suppose someone will clear it up before morning?' He looked at the messy brown liquid doubtfully as if leaving it was a sin of the greatest magnitude.

'Sure to,' I said. 'But I won't be here to know.'

'Don't you belong here, then?' He seemed surprised. 'I thought . . . well, never mind what I thought. Let's go and have some real coffee some-where, or failing that go to the pub.'

'Well, I— '

It would be all right, I reasoned with myself, if I

23

only had an orange juice. You could go in pubs before you were eighteen. It was only the drinking of alcohol that you couldn't do. 'What a good idea!' I enthused.

It wasn't until we were practically inside the pub, warm yellow light spilling out onto the steps as he opened the door for me, that I realised what he meant about not belonging at college. He didn't realise I was still at school.

Oh, well, if he finds out he finds out, I thought philosophically, and smiling as if I did this every night of the week, I went through and sat in the smoky atmosphere.

'Orange juice please,' I said.

'Very wise,' he said. He came back to the table with a pint of beer for him and my glass of orange full of ice tinkling against the sides. It was really too cold for November weather, but it was warm inside and *I* was warm inside and I knew that life was suddenly going to be magical.

I was right. He talked a lot – not saying much, just really nice and friendly. He didn't ask where I was at college or school or anything, though I was scared he was going to all the time. I suppose we were only there for about half an hour, but in one way it seemed like months, not nearly long enough. He stood up to go as soon as I had finished crunching (rather child-ishly, I must admit) the last bits of ice at the bottom of my glass.

'I've been invited to an eighteenth on Saturday. Friend of mine. It'll be a disco, in a pub.' He spoke casually. 'Would you like to come?'

Would I? I don't remember how I answered. I have

a horrible feeling I was all silly and breathless. I
hoped he didn't think I was a complete fool. Then
he said, 'I suppose you'd better get back to your
homework now.'

I can't remember what I said to that either. Probably something flippant. I'd let it out in my conversation after all.

But my heart was singing.

He knows, and he doesn't mind!

Chapter 3

My mother nearly spoiled the whole thing, of course.

No, I didn't say anything about Clive. If I had
she'd have gone on about him coming round to meet
the family and I'd have had a lot of 'little talks' on
sex and love and how did I feel about him deep
down and all that sort of thing. Only she looked
suspiciously at me on Saturday morning – well I
suppose it was a bit unusual, me getting up at nine
o'clock – and then hurriedly changed her face to a
bright smile.

'Well, Frankie – nice to see you so bright and
early!'

'All right, stop being so sarcastic,' I growled.

'No, I mean it. Quite sincerely, folks. How about
taking your father a cup of tea?'

'Isn't he up yet?' I didn't believe it. I thought they

were always up at the crack of dawn, so as not to waste any time when they could be experiencing the world.

'If you got up this time every weekend you'd know he always has a lie in. I have mine on Sunday.'

Well, well, I thought, how very happy and democratic. It didn't make my early morning mood any better though.

'Want some breakfast?' said Mum, still chatty.

Did I? I wasn't sure. I felt slightly sick. I hadn't slept well last night – I was going out with him *tonight*. What was he going to think of me, a schoolgirl? There would be older, more sophisticated, more experienced girls there.

'Breakfast?' I said dully.

'Egg? Or bacon, or sausage, or all three?'

'No, thanks.'

'You ought to have a good protein start to the day, you know,' went on my mother. 'Or would you prefer muesli?'

I shuddered. A choice between nicely grilled bacon, best-quality meaty sausage and/or boiled egg, or nasty chewy whole grains with sour apple grated into it. Why couldn't we have something normal like cornflakes?

'I'll make some tea,' I said abruptly. 'I don't really feel like anything, thanks.'

'But you ought, you know. Breakfast like a king, lunch like a prince, dinner like a pauper,' she quoted from her favourite health food expert.

'That's all very well if you're going to go and be amazingly energetic all day, but I'm not,' I snapped. 'I'm going out to a disco tonight. I'll need to dine like a king to keep my strength up for that.'

She didn't seem to latch on to the sense of that. It was just 'disco' that caught her ears.

'Who are you going with?'

'Oh – somebody.'

'Not Alan?'

'No.' I kept my voice under control, though it was pretty difficult. 'I don't have to go everywhere with Alan.'

'Have you had a little quarrel?' said my mother. 'Never mind. People can't get on all the time. It's quite normal, you know. Nothing to get upset about.'

'I – have – not – had – a – row – with – Alan,' I said, slowly and deliberately. 'And I'm going to the disco with someone else I know. I don't have exclusive rights to Alan. There are other people in the world.'

As you keep saying to me, I thought triumphantly to myself as I marched back upstairs, forgetting that the kettle was on and that I was not only going to have a cup of tea myself but was also meant to be taking one up to my father.

I didn't really want it anyway, I thought, as I surveyed my face in the bathroom mirror, looking anxiously for spots. There was one just starting above my right eyebrow – the worst time it could start – it would be at the peak of perfection tonight. Still, it could be in a worse place. I could probably camouflage it there fairly well. It was the ones on my nose you couldn't do much about, apart from the fact that they seemed to be much more painful there. But there weren't any there today, thank heavens.

My eyes were shadowed with black circles beneath

them. No wonder my mother thought I needed a good protein breakfast or something healthy to brace me up. However, what she didn't know was that the black circles were simply the result of me being too lazy to clean off my experiments with eye-liner last night. The trouble with school is you don't get a chance to wear make-up enough, so when you really need to make a good job of it you often put it on too thick or all wrong. I wondered again whether it would be a good idea to go to college next year instead of staying on at school. Except that college is really dreary and depressing with all that dingy cream paint – where vandalising boots have left any paint. At least school is a bit brighter with posters and artwork done by the talented, which doesn't include me.

Not even on my face, I sighed, scrubbing at the black circles with soap and water and wincing as the soap got into my eyes and stung. I really ought to have bought some cream to get it off with, only when you've only got a limited amount of money it's difficult enough to know whether to lash out on the latest Mary Quant colour or a hair spray or new earrings. Perhaps Mum would have some cream I could borrow.

While I scrubbed I thought about what I could wear. I only had one dress that was at all presentable. It would have to be that. It was quite nice really – a pale green, heavy twill material, straight cut across the shoulders and gathered at the waist. I did, I think, look quite nice in it.

What I really wanted, though, was something a bit more daring. My hair is really brown with sort of red lights in it. I dyed it redder a month ago, and it really looks good. But the green now looks so *safe*. I want bright pink, or a startling pillar box red now, something to make people sit up.

Still, there was no alternative. The green thing would have to do. At least I could do something amazing with my hair and make-up.

I opened my make-up bag and began to experiment again.

I had said I'd meet him on the corner. He'd looked at me with a raised eyebrow which made me panic a bit. I mumbled something about my mother not approving of discos, which sounded, even to my ears, pretty feeble and stupid. But he just nodded and didn't ask any more, thank heavens.

He was there in a car.

It sounds silly, I know, because of course everyone is used to cars. My parents have said often enough, with that tone of exasperation in their voices, that they seem to keep a car purely for my convenience. But none of the other blokes I know have cars. John's motorbike is the nearest thing to luxury transport that any of us know.

It was a little red MG, the kind of thing I always dreamed of travelling in. It was a bit draughty, but who wants the hermetically sealed comfort of a staid family Cortina?

'Punctual,' he said approvingly as I slid into the seat beside him.

'I hate being late,' I said. 'I always think it's such a waste of other people's time. I hate people being late for me — you sit around wondering what's happened to them when you could be doing something else if you weren't fretting about it . . .'

Why did I have to go on *prattling*!

However, he drove on with a half smile on his face, not seeming to mind. Perhaps he understood it was just nerves.

When we got out in the side-street where he had parked, he looked at me with a smile in his eyes which made my heart turn over.

'All right?' he said and linked his arm in mine. I felt a little shiver go down my spine. No wonder Sonia hadn't said anything about him if this was what he did to you!

At least, I thought, I can dance. It would have been awful if he'd invited me to a disco and then stood lamely at the side wondering what to do. And yet when he did say, 'Dance?' I could only nod dumbly and panic. It sounds ridiculous, when I happily dance away at the school or college discos, but I suddenly wasn't sure whether I could!

He said the right thing again, though there was so much noise it was difficult to hear anything but the beat. I didn't mind. The music took a hold of me and I felt marvellous.

And he was really good at disco dancing himself. There aren't many boys I know who are that good. Alan's quite nice to dance with, but he hasn't anything on Clive!

I don't know whose party it was. I never even met him, I don't think. We were in an upstairs room of a pub and there was masses of marvellous food, but that's really all I know about it. He said 'Hello' to a few people, but he always made it quite clear that he'd come with me and he wasn't going to waste time talking to anyone else. I felt wanted, cherished, wonderful!

'Shall we get some food?' he said into my ear after about – I suppose it must have been about half an hour's dancing, but it could just as easily have been half a minute or all eternity. I smiled and followed him to the tables at the side, heaped with mouth-watering pâtés and salads, chicken and ham, flans and quiches. And then there were glorious concoctions of fruit and cakes and cream.

We took our heaped plates to a tiny table. I hadn't realised I was so hungry. It must have been the dancing. If anyone had asked me before then, I would have told them I lived on air.

However, I was all too human, though it all tasted of manna and nectar and all the other foods the gods love.

'This is where I ask all about you,' he said, after a forkful of pâté and salad. ' "Tell me about yourself" is the line, isn't it?'

I began to panic a bit at that.

'I'm not very interesting,' I said hurriedly. 'What about you? What do you do at college, for instance, if the thought of college in a place like this isn't too revolting?'

'Italian.'

I wondered if I'd heard properly. The decibel level was pretty high even in our far corner.

'Pardon?'

'Italian,' he repeated. So I had heard properly.

'But – what for? Have you got Italian relations or something?'

Frankie, when you start talking you really do put your foot in it sometimes.

'No,' he said. 'I'm going to Rome for my holidays this year. It seemed a good idea to know a bit of the language.'

'Oh – yes – I see,' I murmured, a bit dazed. I mean, learning a language because you *want* to is something quite outside my bag. I do French at school, and I was sent to France last year to stay with a family in the hopes of improving it, but it didn't work very well. I think my mother had put me off from the start, telling me to make the most of things and learn how they live and all that. Before I went she'd already begun to make garlic soup and talk longingly of baguettes and pour oily dressing onto our salads when Dad and I sneakily preferred fattening salad cream. I probably might have enjoyed it if I hadn't felt I was being pushed into a French way of living, so I stayed determinedly British.

'So you're only at the college on Thursday evenings?' I said, curiously disappointed. There was even less hope of meeting him on the off-chance, then. I'd probably messed everything up, coming here in a childish dress and talking a load of idiotic nonsense. It was the last time he'd want to take me out. I grimaced into my orange juice – you see, childish drink – and wondered if this was how it had ended for Sonia.

'But I'd rather talk about you,' he murmured, slipping an arm round my shoulders. I shivered at his closeness, though it was boiling hot in the room, and felt strange pricklings down my spine. 'You look marvellous in that green dress, did you know? Prettier than anyone else I can see here.'

I was suddenly, enormously grateful to him, besides being immensely attracted to him. How did he know I was feeling gawky and unassured? Perhaps he didn't, in which case saying he liked my dress was even nicer.

'Tell me about Rome,' I said quickly before he could ask any questions about me. 'Why are you going there?'

'I like Italy,' he said. 'I've been to most of the tourist places and they don't speak English as much as the travel agents say they do, so I thought I'd concentrate on one of the places I liked best and do it properly this time.'

He was light years away from me. I wondered how old he was. But how could you ask?

'Where— ?' The words were whirled away from me. He had taken my fork, set it down on the table and pulled me out onto the floor.

'My favourite record,' he murmured. It seemed to be everyone else's favourite as well, because in the crush I had to press close to him if I didn't want to lose contact completely. He put his arm round my shoulders. I melted. I was in love.

Dreamily, my head against his shoulder, we moved to the music until it ended, then we went back to the still half-full plates we had left at the edge of the room.

'You know, you're really good,' said Clive. It was so sweet to hear that admiration in his voice. 'We must do this more often.'

I felt my smile broaden with happiness, and when we sat down to finish our supper it might have been plastic in my mouth for all I noticed. He had said we must do this more often! He didn't think I was too young, or too naive.

I ate, chatted, listened to him, watched the other people dancing in a haze of smoke. Or was it my eyes going funny? I didn't care. All I wanted was to be aware of him.

Then my tongue let me down again.

'How do you manage to get enough money to go to Italy every year?'

Frankie! Shut up!

But he didn't seem to mind. 'I've got a good job,' he said. 'I've been there four years now. I'd move, but the money's too good.'

Four years! If he'd left school at sixteen he would be twenty now, at least, but if he'd stayed on till he was eighteen he must be twenty-two. My mind boggled. Someone *that* old wanting to come out with me.

It was a bit frightening, in fact. I thought I'd better say nothing else. He couldn't have realised I was still at school after all. That joke about homework must have been just a joke – or he thought I was at the college too, possibly full time or something. Or – no – that was what he had thought at the beginning. Another college, perhaps. The Poly.

'What do you want to do when you leave school?' he said suddenly.

So I was wrong again. I stammered, hesitated. 'Oh, I don't know – college, perhaps – you know . . .'

'Not like that one,' he teased.

'Well— '

'I don't blame you. It is a bit of a dump, isn't it?

34

I'd have done my Italian at the Polytechnic but by the time I got round to it all the courses were filled.'

'I'm glad,' I said, and meant it. It was really the first sensible thing I'd said all evening.

'Thanks,' he said, and he meant it too. Now, I thought, is when he'll ask me to go out with him again next week.

It didn't worry me when he didn't. He had said we must do this again, hadn't he? There was nothing to worry about. I didn't mind when he said it was time to go. It was getting far too noisy in there anyway. I wanted to talk, to . . .

'Where shall I take Cinderella?' he said, teasing, before starting up the car. It was freezing, after the heat in there, and I shivered. When his arm came round me I wished I hadn't, in case he thought I'd done it on purpose so that he should.

'Where?' I stumbled foolishly. No, I was determined not to take him home. I couldn't, I really couldn't, cope with my mother giving her views on sex and open-mindedness. Not tonight. Not ever, with Clive.

'Yes, where? I'm not letting you run home yourself, you know.'

It should have made me feel ecstatically happy, but I just couldn't even let him near our front door.

'Just drop me at the corner,' I babbled. 'Honestly, I'll be all right. You can watch me run home if you like. Wait till I'm inside the door . . .'

He must think I'm totally out of my mind.

'If that's the way you want it.' I could see that eyebrow lift in his amused look. It was amazing, getting to know someone that well, in one evening.

In fact, I don't know why I worried about asking him to drop me on the corner. I might have known he'd understand.

Even the draughty little MG felt warm as he drove through the dark streets, lights from the speeding lampposts reminding me inevitably of those in the disco which had flashed on us only a short time ago. I felt drunk with happiness. Drunk? On orange juice? And he hadn't even nagged about a 'proper drink' like other people might have done. I didn't have to explain that it wasn't that I didn't like alcohol, or didn't know anything about it, that I didn't want to blur any of that evening – any more than my state of mind was blurring it anyway.

Too soon, far too soon, he stopped.

'This do?'

No, I want to drive through the night for ever, was what I wanted to say. 'Yes, that's right,' I said. I fumbled ineffectually at the handle. His arm came across and undid the door but did not go away. I found myself in his arms, and it felt like heaven. The kiss was everything I imagined, and more than I imagined.

I was out of breath when he stopped.

'You'd better go, Cinderella.'

I supposed I'd better.

'Thank you,' I said. Of all the things I could have said. I couldn't think of anything else. I found the handle myself this time and tottered out.

He did as he said he would, and waited till I reached the front door. It was still unlocked. I saw his hand wave as light spilled out from the hall. Then he drove off. That was all.

He hadn't asked me out again, but he would. He liked me enough to give me that kiss, to say nice things about my dancing, my clothes. I would never throw that dress away: it would be my favourite until it hung in shreds round my ankles.

Never mind that he hadn't said it. He would phone tomorrow. Or the next day. And in any case I'd see him on Thursday. If I did my homework quickly I'd go to the swimming pool — no, that would make my hair a mess — perhaps I'd play table tennis with Alan for a while, if he wanted to. It didn't matter what I did. I didn't need an excuse to go there. He'd seen me there often enough already. And then there would be the next day, the next . . .

Chapter 4

What do you do with Sunday when there's nothing to do but sit and wait for someone to telephone?

I got up early. Again. And met Dad downstairs, making tea for Mum. He made some cracks like Mum had yesterday when I said I was surprised to see him.

'Oh, all right,' I growled. '*Sorry* I don't get up and bring you both tea in bed.'

'I rather enjoy my pottering around on my own on Sundays,' he said mildly.

'I suppose I've spoiled it,' I snarled.

'No. Nice to see you.'

'For a change, I suppose you mean.'

He merely smiled and poured me some tea. He didn't even tell me to take up Mum's. You can't win with parents.

Why I was in such a temper I really don't know. Last night had been perfect. I should have been basking in its warmth, curling my toes down to the bottom of my warm bed, remembering how we had danced, remembering the nice things he'd said about my clothes, my hair, my eyes . . .

My parents' bedroom is right on top of the kitchen. I sat shivering slightly in my old, tattered dressing gown, feet bare because my old slippers had worn out and I had spent all my clothes money on a pair of boots. Their voices murmured above me, sounding happy and contented. I envied them.

I was jealous. I wanted to be with Clive now, this minute. I didn't want to have to wait till he phoned, till the next time we could meet.

But it wasn't that. Not really. I didn't want to admit it, but it was still there, in the back of my mind.

He hadn't said anything. He hadn't said he would phone. Apart from that time – and as the day wore on, I became more and more convinced that I had imagined it – that time he'd said 'We must do this again', he hadn't said anything else about meeting again. The kiss, surely that meant something? That kept me going for another half hour. But wasn't this a thing about men? They could kiss and forget as easily as changing a shirt.

I moped about the house until my mother started

shouting at me.

'Frankie, if you can't stop mooning go away and moon in your bedroom! I don't know what's got into you today!'

'I'm no different from usual,' I lied.

'If you can't find anything to do then I'll find something for you,' she threatened.

'Like what?'

I didn't mean to be rude. It was just that I couldn't stand being criticised today.

'All the things you should have done and haven't,' she snapped back. 'I don't suppose you've done all your homework yet, have you?'

'Surprisingly, I have,' I answered.

'Then I don't suppose you've done it properly.'

I stared. This wasn't like my mother. It was her philosophy that if you didn't do it it was your own fault, and you had to take the consequences.

'I don't suppose I have,' I said. I didn't really care. 'So what? It's my O levels. My life.'

Since this was what she was always saying to me, she couldn't really argue with that. She just sighed with exasperation and went off somewhere.

When Clive phones I shall be quite happy, I wanted to say to her. But then I'd have to confess who I'd been out with and she'd want me to bring him home. I nearly did, only in the middle of the afternoon she came up and said, 'You know, Frankie, if there's anything wrong you've only got to say. We can discuss it together.'

'Wrong?' I said brightly. 'Why should there be anything wrong? Don't be silly.'

She looked at me doubtfully, but didn't go on

about it. Funny. She was very quiet for the rest of the day. In the end I just went off to my bedroom and read a book. I couldn't concentrate, but then I couldn't really concentrate on anything. I was listening for the telephone all the time. Twice I sneaked downstairs to see if the receiver was still on its cradle. I wanted to ring the exchange to see if it was out of order, but they'd have noticed.

He didn't phone at all that day.

'What's the matter with you, Frances?'

I jerked back to attention and history.

'Sorry, what?' I said, which only made the whole form yell with laughter. Even though it was so near O levels, we still played up Miss Higgins. I don't know why she ever became a teacher – she was tallish, gawky, flustered, her hair always falling over the place. The most notable thing about her was that she always wore brown. And you could do what you liked with her. I suppose nobody cared much whether they got history or not. Sometimes I felt sorry for her, but honestly, she shouldn't have been there at all, hating it so much. It was really her own fault.

Anyway, I found it difficult enough to concentrate on things that mattered, let alone history. But somehow, that morning, I felt even sorrier for poor Miss Higgins. Perhaps she had a lover who didn't phone her. It would be enough to put anyone off teaching a load of idiots like us. I sat at the back, because I can't see too well if I'm near the front and I simply refuse to wear glasses. My mother thinks they'd suit me, but if I can't get contact lenses then I'll just be blind. Anyway, in front of me I could see even Carol Giles, the quietest one of the lot of us, passing notes to her friend across the desks. And John Alder, who, although he was one of the worst of us last year, wants to get all his O levels so much that even he shuts up in Miss Higgins' lesson, had got so fed up with behaving that he'd fitted a wodge of paper, well soaked in old flower water, to the end of a flexible ruler and was aiming it towards the front.

'Oh, shut up, John,' I said loudly, and poked him in the back with my pencil so that he missed his aim. The smelly package fell down Wayne Derrick's neck and of course he started shouting.

The most unfair thing was she gave *me* an order mark, when all I was trying to do was stick up for her and stop the others from playing her up. There's no justice.

And the rest of the day seemed nothing but people nagging. 'Wake up, Frances,' or, 'I thought you had more brain than that, Frances,' in that tone of icy sarcasm which seemed specially reserved for teachers.

Sonia was all distant and funny too. I tried to get back to our old footing at break, asking if she was going to the college to swim this week, but she only muttered something inaudible and slouched off with Caz. I actually nearly felt like crying at that point. I wanted to ask her if Clive had phoned her, or if she'd had to hang about at home listening for the first 'ting' before a proper ring, rushing to get there before her parents, only to find it was some business colleague of her father or the insurance man or someone equally boring. And I wanted to ask if she'd been as *crushed* when it wasn't him — as if it had been raining for a month and the sun almost came through the clouds then went back again for another month.

I kept trying to tell her I'd been out with him on Saturday. I thought once I'd got that over, and she didn't mind about it, then I could talk to her. But somehow every time I started to say anything she'd change the subject or pretend she was doing something else.

I was really glad to get home after that even though there hadn't been a phone call. Of course I knew there wouldn't have been one, not while I was at school, but you can't help hoping, can you? It was one of Mum's days when she's at home, and I thought perhaps he might have phoned while she was out shopping or something. It was always possible. And there was a whole evening left.

I did my homework quickly – to my mother's surprise. I could see her wanting to make some sarcastic comment, but she didn't. Just as well – I'd had enough of that at school today. So I suppose when Alan turned up later on it wasn't surprising that she greeted him with cries of joy.

I hung about the kitchen while they rabbitted on about the latest political horror, Alan's mum's new job, how to cook skirt of beef and whether girls of fourteen should be allowed to have the Pill.

'What do you think, Frankie?' asked my mother. Her eyes were all shining with the pleasure of discussion.

'How should I know,' I growled. I didn't *want* to know. All I wanted to know was whether Clive was going to ring me up. Even if I wanted to talk about these mind-blowing problems I would still have that at the back of my thoughts all the time.

'It's something you might well have to think about at some time,' said my mother, looking hurt.

'Well, I don't want to just now,' I said. 'Can we change the subject, please?'

'I don't know what's come over her,' said my mother to Alan, who was looking on at this exchange with a slightly amused expression on his face. I could have kicked both of them. 'She's been grumpy all weekend.'

'Must be the time of the month,' said Alan.

'Oh, for crying out *loud*!' I shouted. 'Can't I be grumpy without it being for any special reason? Can't I be grumpy just because I *feel* like it, and with nothing to do with my age or the time of year or the time of the month?'

This was a mistake. It's just the sort of thing my mother likes to get her teeth into. I could see her getting ready for a nice complicated discussion, but I really couldn't cope.

'I'm going upstairs,' I said. 'If you want any help you know where I am. Or Alan can do it, if you're so stuck on having a nice quarrel.'

'I think she needs your company more than I do,' Mum said to Alan. I cringed mentally – trying to shove us together again. Well, how mistaken could she be! All the same, I did need him. You can't be friends with someone all your life without knowing how they think and feel, and I really wanted his opinion.

'Come on, then,' I said crossly, because it looked as if my mother had got her own way again. 'We'll go into the sitting room – if it's warm. I'm frozen solid today, even if the weather is supposed to be warmer.'

'It's because of the humidity, damp always makes you feel colder ... ' I heard her say as we went through.

'What are you cross about, then?' said Alan as soon as we were out of earshot.

'Cross? Me?'

'Oh, shut up,' he said. 'I know you. What are you cross about?'

'I went out with Clive on Saturday,' I said.

'That's nice. Well?'

He seemed sort of distant. It was funny, not like Alan at all. I thought he'd be all interested and want to know everything, right from the word go, like he does if I go to the cinema with Sonia or to a party when he hasn't come with us.

'Well — well I thought he might have phoned and he hasn't.'

I didn't know what to say. He'd thrown me with that cold 'Well?'

'What's wrong with you all?' I demanded. 'Here's Sonia not saying a word at school, and all you can say is 'Well?' and look sullen! What's wrong with him? Do you all know something that I don't? Because if you do you'd better tell me.'

'I don't know anything,' said Alan. He stared down at his fingernails, which was another thing he never does. He always looks you directly in the face when he talks. I've never seen him all shifty like this. I began to worry.

'Are you sure? He hasn't got a prison record or anything?'

'Not as far as I know.'

'Alan, come *on*! What *is* it?'

'I've told you. I don't know anything about him. Why should I? I don't know every single person at college.'

'He's only there on Thursday evenings,' I owned.

'There you are, then.'

'What do you mean, there you are, then? Surely somebody knows something about him?'

'Quite probably,' he said, 'only I'm not one of them. And I'm not that interested in finding out either. It seems to me that you're the one that's in the best position for that.'

Honestly, he could be so exasperating I could kill him sometimes.

'You're worse than my mother,' I said.

'And there's another thing,' he said, still in that cold, hard voice that I don't remember him ever using before. 'I think the way you speak to your mother is quite appalling. She's trying to help you and all you do is answer back or ridicule her or sulk . . .'

He hadn't finished, but I could feel anger and resentment boiling up like a kettle and it all came whistling out.

'*Me* answer back and ridicule her! You've got a cheek, haven't you? What right have you got to tell me how I ought to behave to my own mother? You come here and take over the conversation, argue with her, say she's wrong . . .'

'But that's the way she likes it,' said Alan, his eyes glinting dangerously.

'How do you know? Perhaps she'd prefer you to agree with her one day. I think it's disgusting the way you come here and eat our food and drink our coffee and then have the cheek to tell me off.'

'You can come to our house any time you like,' he said. The calmness was beginning to crack, to my great satisfaction. 'Why don't you? I always come here.'

'Have I ever invited you?' I snapped. 'You just turn up, whether we want you or not. A bit big-headed, don't you think?'

'I certainly won't come here again if you feel that way,' said Alan, and his voice rose to a pitch where it sounded as if it might go soprano at any moment. 'I never want to be where I'm not welcome. If I ever do come here it will be because your mother has invited me, and I shall make quite sure that you're not at home at the same time.'

'That suits me!' I yelled. 'And if you've got any more criticisms keep them to yourself. I don't want you discussing me with my mother behind my back.'

He was already on his way out, but he stopped at that and turned round. Guilty conscience, I suppose. 'You don't believe I would do a thing like that, do you?' he said.

'It's true, isn't it?'

'If that's what you want to think,' he shrugged.

'You're not denying it, then,' I sneered.

'I can't see you believing anything I say while you're in this mood,' he said insufferably.

'*Me*! Who started it, may I ask? It wasn't me doing all the criticising.'

'No,' he said quietly. 'No, it wasn't.'

'Well then.' I felt my head go back on my neck and it wasn't just because he's a bit taller than me and I have to look up at him. It was as if my chin had to go that high to stop my eyes leaking tears. I wasn't going to let him see I cared that we were quarrelling.

He shut the door with such exaggerated care that I half expected it to slam of its own accord out of frustration. I was still holding my head up, because after he'd gone I really felt the tears were going to have their own way. I ran upstairs to my room. I could cry then, where nobody would be likely to see.

It was shatteringly awful, not just because I'd had a quarrel. I don't mind the odd row, and have had many with Sonia, which just leave me blazing for an hour or two, then we make it up. Or we have until lately. It was because I've never had a quarrel with Alan before — not since we were small and quarrelled over rights in our toys, which were so mixed up before Alan's family moved that we never quite knew who owned what.

It wasn't fair. I lay on my bed and buried my head in the pillows. Everybody criticised their parents. It was normal. Sonia goes on at hers.

I could have taken it from Dad, or if I'd been rude to him, I'd have listened to my mother if she'd told me off about it. But Alan. It was *him* saying anything that I really hated.

And only because I wanted to know about Clive. Why should that have made him in such a temper unless there was something wrong about Clive?

I couldn't believe there was anything. He was too nice. He was kind to me, said my clothes looked good and that I was beautiful. A whole lot more than Alan had ever said to me.

I thought I'd really rather listen to Clive than Alan

any day.

If only I could get the chance.

I ran home every day that week, hoping there'd be a message, and I hung about the house, not going anywhere, each evening.

'You're getting a lot of work done,' said my mother brightly on Wednesday night when I emerged from my room to watch a late film on television.

'Um?' I said noncommittally.

'Up in your room as soon as you get home. It's nice to see you're getting down to things. Is it panic, or is it more interesting now?'

'Oh, panic, I expect,' I said, and immediately felt guilty again. I hadn't done any work at all. Not school work. My rough book was full of scribbled poems, all bad, most crossed out, crying out my need for Clive and how much I wanted to hear from him.

And it had only been four days. The longest of my life.

But life went on lengthening itself even further. He wasn't even at college on Thursday. That is, he might have been at his Italian lecture, but he certainly didn't come to the common room to fight with the coffee machine, nor did he show his face anywhere where I was: along the corridors, in the spectator part of the swimming pool, nor, as far as I could tell, in the pool itself – though it's pretty difficult to identify anyone in a swimming pool unless they've got wasp-striped trunks or something equally distinctive.

The very worst day was Saturday. I even had hopes up till seven o'clock that evening, but after eight I knew, positively knew, that I wasn't going to hear from him at all.

My life was shattered.

He was too experienced. He was too old for me.

I thought I'd behaved pretty well up to now. A whole week waiting, not getting annoyed at anything. (So there, Alan.)

On Sunday evening, after tea, when I was doing my dutiful bit of clearing up, my mother said, 'Where's Alan these days? I haven't seen him for a week.'

Now was the time to be really cutting, to say something which would make it quite clear that I wasn't under the same delusions as my mother, that however cosily Alan and I had been brought up together, this didn't mean we were going to be cosily together for the rest of our lives.

Instead, I burst into tears and ran from the room.

Chapter 5

It was the worst thing I could have done, of course. My mother instantly assumed that it was because of Alan not coming round that I was all upset. I kept telling her it wasn't anything to do with him, but I couldn't tell her who it was to do with.

'You know, people do have little quarrels and upsets,' she said after school on Monday, when I arrived home like a bedraggled rat – not just because of the rain.

'Oh yes?' I said, as if she was talking about someone else. I fought to get my coat off quickly so that I could disappear upstairs.

'If you want to talk about it, I'm always here,' she said.

'I know you're always here!' I said under my breath.

'What?' She was already halfway into the sitting room, and I didn't want to say it again louder — not because she'd be annoyed, but because she'd be understanding, and I just couldn't cope with that.

It was a relief to lie on my bed and just cry. Sonia had been awful all day. I didn't seem to have any friends left at all. And I didn't even seem to be able to work properly either. Not that I care much about that, but there are some things I'm quite interested in and today they might have been motorcycle maintenance or dishmop mechanics for all I understood of them.

And it went on like that all week. It's funny, isn't it, that when you want the time to go slowly, like that Saturday night with Clive so long ago, it goes as fast as Concorde. Then when you wish Monday to Thursday would disappear like ice cream on a hot day, each second, each minute, each hour drags in a deadly lifelessness.

So slowly that I almost forgot it was Thursday when it did arrive. I came home from school. I took off my coat. I carried my bag of books upstairs. It was just another day like all the rest. I didn't even wonder whether anyone had telephoned. I didn't think it was very likely. But I was prepared to wait for it to ring all evening again, as I had for the past

– how many evenings? And when my mother asked why Alan hadn't been round again, it was just part of the whole dreariness and I didn't even want to complain or cry or anything.

I watched myself do a French translation in a dull torpor. It was finished and I started on maths. Dad called from downstairs that tea was ready. I could smell something delicious, but instead of my taste buds making my mouth water with desire, I felt sick; not hungry at all.

'Thought you'd be out today as usual,' my father said as I pushed the smallest forkful of soufflé into my mouth, hoping it wouldn't choke me on its way down.

'Today?' I said vaguely. No, there was too much. I put the fork down and carefully cut the centimetre cube in half.

'Swimming, or something? Isn't that usually where you go on Thursdays?'

'She's upset about something,' interrupted my mother. 'Don't worry her. I think she's had a row with Alan, but she won't let on.'

'Oh, well, we all have quarrels,' said Dad. 'No relationship ever works properly without a row or two, isn't that right, Elizabeth?'

Instead of reflecting on how corny all these clichés sounded, I stopped with the half centimetre of soufflé halfway to my mouth and said, 'Swimming? What day is it?'

'Thursday,' said my mother. 'We've been trying to tell you for the last half hour.'

'Thursday!' I shrieked. 'Why didn't somebody *tell* me!'

They had that long-suffering look on their faces as I ran from the table and grabbed my swimming things from the cupboard under the stairs. Thursday. Clive's Italian class. The possibility of seeing him. My heart began singing as I ran along the dark streets, my plastic carrier bumping at my sides.

It wasn't until I was actually in the pool that it hit me.

Suppose he didn't want to see me?

Suppose if he saw me he was horribly embarrassed and turned and walked away? That would be so much worse than not seeing him that I nearly got out of the pool and ran home, dripping. But Caroline and Jane were there, and if I'd done anything daft like that it would have been round school in five minutes flat, and I just couldn't bear that. So I stuck it out, even when a crowd of little boys of about ten came and started swimming underneath me and grabbing my toes.

We stayed in for about an hour, which was quite long enough for me. All I wanted to do was crawl home, but you can't, when Caz is around. Usually it's great when we all get together and gossip in the common room, but this evening it was the last place I wanted to be.

'Did you ever see that bloke again?' asked Caz curiously.

My heart began to pound. I was sure everybody could see it. I couldn't control my breathing either, so that it was in a kind of squeak that I said, 'What bloke?' and had to turn it into a cough, pretending that my machine-chocolate drink had gone down the wrong way.

'I'm sure they put crumbs in it on purpose,' said Caz suspiciously, looking down at the muddy dregs in her paper cup. 'That bloke – you know – came and talked to us that evening you were waiting for Alan to win his match and he didn't.'

'He wasn't half in a bad temper,' agreed Jane. 'Anyone want more of this stuff?'

'No, thanks,' I shuddered. 'I don't know what they've done with it today. I mean, it's usually only after swimming it tastes like anything drinkable at all.'

'Perhaps they've changed the chlorine,' suggested Caroline. 'Though it tasted just as vile to me.'

'Must have changed the chocolate, then,' I said. 'Perhaps it only tastes all right when you *haven't* been swallowing gallons of chlorine.'

But I might have known I couldn't put her off. When Caz wants to know something, no amount of changing the subject will put her off.

'That bloke. The good-looking one. I thought he fancied you.'

I thought so too, I thought sadly.

'Oh, him.'

If it had been a week ago I'd have told her all about him. I wouldn't have been able not to. But since he hadn't phoned – since it looked as though whatever he might have fancied, he didn't now – I didn't want to say anything.

'I thought . . . ' began Caz.

'Didn't he go out with Sonia once?' said Jane.

'Yes,' I said quickly. 'You know, last year, ages ago.'

'Oh, well, I suppose he came over to see her,' said

Caz, as if she were disappointed. 'I really thought it was you he fancied, Frankie.'

'Sorry,' I said brightly. 'Must have been you.'

I was beginning to panic. It was about the time that the evening classes finished, and if I wasn't careful he'd be walking into the dismal room. I couldn't bear even to wonder whether he'd ignore me or come over and talk to the three of us. I wanted to go, but if I went Caz would make some comment and it would be even worse. I supposed I'd have to stick it out and hope he just waved in a friendly way and walked off.

The thing I really couldn't stand would be if he came over and talked to us and then walked off.

I needn't have worried. We stayed there for another half hour, and every time the swing doors opened my glance swivelled round. It was with a mixture of relief and disappointment that I saw it was someone else each time. The room filled up with people, noise and cigarette smoke and then emptied again almost as quickly.

'I suppose I'd better get back and finish my homework,' said Jane with a sigh, getting up from the hard seat and hoisting her striped beach bag over her shoulder.

'Done mine,' said Caz smugly. 'I'm really looking forward to the day when I leave and haven't got to do it any more. Life must hold something more worthwhile than O level maths.'

'*If* we ever get it,' I agreed. 'Where did you get that bag, Jane? I want one!'

I kept talking strenuously as we wandered out. Just in case we should happen to bump into him. I didn't want to be silent at the time, gawping like a stranded fish. I wanted him to think I didn't care, that I wasn't getting in touch with him because I wasn't that keen on his company either, and that I would be perfectly distantly friendly if that was the way he wanted it, though I wasn't going to cry my eyes out if he didn't.

But he didn't, of course, cross our path in that short walk from the common room to the road outside, and I didn't, of course, feel anything like that at all.

I thought my heart would probably break.

'Frankie,' said my mother later that evening, 'if you fiddle about with that curtain much more it will fall to pieces.'

'Oh, *sorry*,' I said. 'I seem to get criticised for every small thing these days.'

The phone rang, and I rushed to it.

'For you,' I said dully, holding the receiver out to my mother.

She took it, with a glance which said volumes – you know, that tight-lipped 'I'd-better-not-shout-at-her-she-needs-understanding' sort of look. I just wish she would shout sometimes – you wouldn't feel so guilty about being awkward and bloody-minded then.

'I wonder if you need some extra vitamins,' she said when she'd finished talking on the telephone. 'You teenagers need extra protein and vitamins, just at the time you refuse to eat properly.'

'Oh, *Mum*,' I said just as Dad came through, looking a bit vague as he does when he's still thinking about work.

'That was Jim on the phone,' said my mother, immediately switching from me to him. 'A folk concert next Wednesday – do you fancy going? I must say it sounded rather nice. Your favourite singer.'

'What? Muggsy Bond?' At least that was what it sounded like to me. They've got really weird names, these singers my parents go in for. They met at a folk club, so I suppose this is why they keep going to them. I can't stand them. I mean, sometimes they do songs about the bomb and that, and I suppose I think that's a good thing. But I don't think anybody's going to listen to them in a folk club. Anyway, the music is boring – there's no beat. Nothing you could dance to.

But they were all excited about this concert next Wednesday, and I was feeling more and more miserable because there was nowhere I wanted to go and there was nobody to go with even if I wanted to.

Eventually they noticed I wasn't in the brightest of moods.

'Cheer up, Frankie,' said my father.

'She's been like this all week,' said my mother, definitely exasperated this time. 'I keep telling her we're only too happy to talk if she's worried about anything.'

'"Does she take sugar?"' I quoted. 'I am here, you know. I'm not deaf, or out of my mind or anything.'

'Well, can we help?' Dad looked a bit lost. I think even he gets embarrassed at my mother when she tries to get to the heart of things.

'No, thanks,' I said, and I heard my mother sigh.

The phone went. Again. I didn't rush this time. It would look too obvious. But my mother smiled and looked over at me.

'For you,' she said.

'Me?' I said, my heart leaping. I nearly snatched it from her and tried to will them both to go away.

'It's Sonia.' What a let down! What did she want anyway? She hadn't spoken to me for days.

'Hello. What do you want?'

'Charming,' said Sonia's voice. 'I'll go away if that's how you feel. I was just feeling fed up and wondered if you'd like to come round. But if you don't want to there are other people.'

She tried to make it sound as if she was joking, but I knew better. I nearly said I hadn't finished my homework yet and that I needed to revise anyway, but then I thought at least it would be *someone* to talk to, even if I couldn't talk about Clive.

And at her house, if she was in a good mood and if her mother had been baking her delicious scones or cakes, she might even tell me about Clive.

'Well?' She sounded impatient.

I hadn't realised how long my thoughts had taken.

'Right,' I said. 'I'll come over.'

'And if you've got that French translation done can I have a look at it and see if I've got the same as you?'

'I knew there was some reason why you wanted me,' I said. 'I knew it couldn't be just because you wanted to see your old friend.'

'Oh, shut up,' said Sonia. 'In half an hour?'

'See you.'

'Well that's nice,' said my mother. 'I haven't seen Sonia for a long time. Or any of your other friends, come to think of it. Is everything all right at school?

No difficulties?'

I couldn't tell her it was because of her that my friends don't come round. She honestly doesn't realise what it's like for me, having to face them afterwards, making fun of her.

'No,' I said shortly. 'We're all working for our mocks. Nobody goes out much just now.'

'It's nice to know you're actually doing some work,' said my father.

I gave him a dirty look.

'We'd probably do more if we didn't get nagged about it,' I said, which I realised was unfair because they don't, usually.

'We're only concerned for your future, you know,' he said mildly. 'You can be a dustman if you really want to, only I don't happen to think you'd really want to.'

'Be lucky to get a dustman's job these days,' I said. 'It's going to be a matter of pure luck if I land a job at all, I should think.'

'In that case all the more reason for getting your exams and finding out what sort of thing you enjoy if you're going to be sitting around at home for the rest of your life,' he said.

But I'd heard it all before – it was another of Alan's favourite discussions with my mother. It wasn't that I didn't agree with them. I just wanted it to be my own idea if I did anything.

'Well, I've got to go,' I said. 'I won't be late. If anyone rings . . . '

'Tell him you're at Sonia's,' said my mother with a grin.

That was the last thing I wanted. I nearly shrieked.

She'd nearly caught me . . .

'But nobody will,' I assured her, afraid that I was right. 'There isn't any "him" anyway.'

I was almost sure, by now, that what I said was true. Perhaps I could get Sonia to say something, to find out if I was right.

It was nice, to begin with, to be at Sonia's again. Her mother had been baking, and her house was filled with the scent of spicy buns and fruit cake. Ours always seems to have a faint tinge of garlic and beans all the time – certainly not sweet cakes because Mum thinks they're bad for you. I don't care if they are; when Sonia's mum bakes, I'm as greedy as Sonia herself.

We stuffed ourselves contentedly while Sonia checked her French against mine, and we decided that one of us must be wrong but we weren't sure who. Suddenly it didn't matter, and we were gossiping away as if nothing had come between us these last few weeks, when she suddenly said, 'Who's that girl Alan's been going out with?'

I was freezing cold, all of a sudden.

'Alan?' I said. 'How should I know?'

'I thought he was a friend of yours.'

Talk about bitchy! So that was why she asked me round – to make me upset. Well, little did she know it wasn't going to upset me at all.

'He's a friend, yes,' I agreed, 'but I don't have any control over his girlfriends, any more than I have over your boyfriends.' This was meant to be a dig about last year, when she'd cut me out of her life completely during her Clive period.

'I just wondered,' she said.

A stony silence grew up between us like a wall, and the spicy cakes, which half an hour ago had seemed light as gossamer, began to weigh down my stomach like rocks.

'Only John knows this Julie, so I thought you'd know her as well.'

'Why should I?' I said. 'I haven't seen Alan for ages anyway. I think he must have gone off my mum like you lot have.' I was trying to joke. 'Who is this Julie anyway?'

'Someone at college, he says. We've seen her at the swimming pool sometimes. That one with black hair. Slim. Pretty.'

Thank you, Sonia. You know how to make a person feel good.

'I expect I'd remember if she was pointed out to me,' I said, trying to sound disinterested.

I suddenly didn't want to stay there any more. I didn't want to know her opinion about Clive either, even if she wanted to tell me anything. It would only be bitchy too, not at all like him. I mean, you can't be objective about a bloke if he's given you the push, can you? Although it seemed laughable, we ought to be the best of friends since he seemed to have done the same to both of us.

I just wished she hadn't managed it for longer. I did think I was a bit better-looking. I probably talked too much – my mother's influence.

I started gathering up my French books and packed them into my bag.

'Say thanks to your mother for the cakes, Sonia,' I said, standing up.

'Have you got to go?' she said, looking

disappointed.

'Just remembered one homework I haven't done,' I said.

'You can do it here,' said Sonia. You could see she didn't believe me. She knows as well as I do what homework I've got since we're both doing the same exams.

'Left my books at home,' I said. 'Anyway, I said I wouldn't be late.'

She got up from the floor where we'd been sitting in front of the fire and picked up the empty, crumby plate.

'I didn't know you didn't know about Alan,' she said.

Like hell, I thought.

'See you tomorrow,' was all I could say, and let myself out.

I'd like to be able to say that while I was out Clive phoned. I don't know what I'd have done if he had – cried all night, I suppose, in case he never did it again. But he didn't. And I cried all night, just the same.

I've never had any sympathy for people who commit suicide. It always seems to me to be the easy way out. But after another day at school with everyone asking *me* about Alan's girlfriend, and Sonia not speaking again because she thought I'd gone off in a huff – which I had – I felt so miserable on the way home that I was almost seriously thinking about the cool dark waters of the canal. Alternatively, and probably better, I could just run away from home. I was almost enjoying myself, thinking where I'd go, and whether I'd let anyone know or not and if I did, how soon. I didn't really hear the car horn behind me, or if I did, I didn't take any notice of it. It's quite a busy street, and people are always honking at doddery drivers or idiots who come bombing out of the side road without looking properly. It went on hooting, and I was beginning to feel quite irritated, when the car drew up just in front of me and waited till I walked the three or four steps to the front of the car.

I don't know how I managed those three steps. My bones had turned to meringue. I had to tread carefully in case they shattered.

I was painfully conscious of my school uniform.

'Hi, Cinderella.'

'Clive!' I couldn't get the wobbliness out of my voice. I hope he didn't notice that, or the shaking of my hands.

'If you'd told me your surname, Cinderella,' he said through the open window, 'I'd have been able to phone you and tell you I had to go away on business for a fortnight. Sorry we didn't get our dancing last weekend. What about tomorrow? Are you free?'

Was I free! My hands still shook, but the wobble in my voice steadied, though the bubble of elation which was threatening to burst out of my chest nearly ruined it again. He hadn't known my surname. He didn't even know where I lived, really, because of me making him leave me at the corner. But there would be time to think about these things later. Just at this moment I had to answer a question.

'Love to,' I said, in what I hoped was a suitably nonchalent tone.

'At Jocasta's, tomorrow?'

'Jocasta's? But ...' Stop butting, you feeble-minded moron. 'Er – what time?'

'Eight, say? I suppose I'll have to pick you up on the corner again!'

He was teasing, but he still didn't seem to mind.

'At the corner, eight o'clock,' I agreed, laughing.

'And tell your parents – if you've got any, Miss Incognito – that you'll be late.'

'Right,' I said. 'I'll tell them not to wait up.'

He pulled his head back and revved up the little MG with a noisy roar.

I watched it disappear down the road and suddenly the world was alight.

Chapter 6

Tomorrow. Jocasta's. And I had nothing to wear.

I couldn't wear that green thing again, and besides, even though he had been nice about it last time, it had seemed terribly unsophisticated compared to the things other people were wearing. Jocasta's was different, though – the girls didn't wear way-out clothes, but terribly sexy things, as far as I could make out from what I'd heard.

It was one of these night clubs that everybody goes to. I must say, I'd envied some of the girls in our class at school who have managed to get there one way or another. You're supposed to be at least eighteen, but so long as you look old enough you can get in without having to provide a birth certificate or anything, like you do on the bus if you've got a student ticket.

In my room I got out all the money I possessed, even rummaging amongst my earrings and junk drawers in case there were stray pennies which I occasionally found when I wasn't looking. One twopence and two pennies. Not exactly riches.

I still had a few pounds of my clothes allowance. How I wished I hadn't squandered a lot of it on those boots which I didn't really like at the time and liked even less as I wore them. And I'd already borrowed half my next allowance. My parents didn't like doing this much, and they'd be dead against lending anything even more in advance. Perhaps, because this was a special occasion, they'd let me, just for once.

But of course I couldn't. I'd have to give them all the reasons why, and I knew they wouldn't think much of me going to Jocasta's under age. They're funny that way – liberal as anything, you'd think, until it comes to little points of law like what age you can go to a pub or X films at the cinema. They say that the law was made for our protection and if we don't like it we should go about changing it in the proper way, not by breaking it whenever we found it inconvenient. That way leads to anarchy, my father says. That's one of the things Alan and my mother argue about constantly. Me – I just stay out of it and wish someone would change the law for me *now* when I want it changed.

But the pressing problem just now was how I could

get enough money to buy something to wear to Jocasta's. Then I had a sudden thought. There was the money I'd been saving for my mother's birthday present. She'd wanted a sandwich toaster for ages, and although I knew it would cost a lot, I wanted to get it for her. So I'd been saving for the last six months, putting some money by each week into the post office. I could put it back from my next clothes allowance. Some of it. Or borrow from Dad for the birthday present. I ignored the fact that although he'd gladly lend it, he'd want to know why I hadn't saved up beforehand. I didn't want to think things out too logically.

So on Saturday morning I startled my mother again by getting up for breakfast – and startled her even more by eating the egg and wholemeal toast she cooked for me.

'It's nice to see you eating, Frankie,' she said, standing with the mug of tea she was about to take up to my father. 'Got a long day ahead?'

Sometimes my mother forgets her understanding and takes refuge in a snide sarcasm. I ignored it. I suppose she hadn't had a good night, or something. We daughters can be quite understanding too.

It seemed a good enough moment to tell her I'd be late tonight, before I lost my nerve.

'Oh, Sonia and I are going to a party tonight. We'll be back late. Don't wait up.'

It was frighteningly easy how the lies managed to slide off my tongue.

'Are you coming back with anyone responsible?' she said, and I gaped.

'I thought you said the other day that I had to be

responsible for myself?' I argued. 'How can I practise being responsible if you're going to nursemaid me all the time?'

'Yes, I suppose you're right,' she said. 'It's just — oh, mothers find it difficult to remember their babies are growing up.'

'Mum! That's sickly.'

She grinned suddenly. 'Yes, it is, isn't it? Sorry. Have a nice time, and I promise we won't wait up.'

It left me feeling guilty, since I wasn't, I suppose, being responsible at all, lying about where I was going and who I was going with. Still, I reasoned, if it wasn't for the fact that she would frighten the life out of anyone but Alan by her insistence on 'talking about things', there wouldn't have been any need for deception.

I still felt guilty, especially when I saw the prices of the sort of dress I knew I'd have to buy for Jocasta's. Mum's birthday present was going to have to be a Christmas present, if there was enough left even then, for Christmas was only a month away. My December allowance would only just cover it, and I wouldn't be able to get away with these shoes for much longer.

I wished Sonia was with me. She and I always got on well shopping for clothes. I wanted her advice. I wanted her to say that the cheaper one which I liked would be just the thing. But she wasn't with me, and I bought a red silky thing, a bit lower in the neck than I'd ever worn before, and a bit clingy round the hips. It was probably exactly right for Jocasta's, but it wasn't me.

I felt even worse about it when I got home. I

66

managed to smuggle it in without my mother noticing. Dad saw me as I was walking upstairs, but all he said was, 'Spending a fortune again?'

'Yes,' I said, quite truthfully, and managed to laugh as I took the stairs two at a time before he asked to have a look.

When I tried it on in front of my mirror I knew it had been a mistake. I looked like a pop star at the Royal Variety Performance.

Well, that was what you were supposed to look like at Jocasta's. Perhaps I wouldn't feel so bad when I was actually there. I'd wanted to look older and sophisticated, hadn't I? I hoped it was an over-eighteen night: sometimes they had a limit of twenty-one, but surely he wouldn't have asked me to one of those. I thought I could probably pass for eighteen, if I was lucky and the make-up I had practised so hard with was sophisticated enough, but twenty-one would be pushing it a bit.

That evening I refused supper, saying we'd get food there, and I stayed upstairs until it was nearly time to go, afraid my parents would ask questions. My stomach was churning by the time I was ready to go.

It went on feeling peculiar when I met him on the corner. I didn't really know about that dress. I wished I'd asked Sonia – somebody – anybody. Suppose, when I took my coat off, it was all wrong. I'd loved the colour with my hair – it had worked, the way I always thought red would – but had I been too daring? I almost wept with apprehension.

Then when we had parked, and he'd come round to my side to open the door and let me out, that look of his made my heart melt all over again.

'All right?' he said, as he had the first time.

I smiled back at him. Well, even if I wasn't dressed right, even if they threw me out of Jocasta's, yes, I was all right. Very much so.

And they didn't make any comment about my age at all, though I was decidedly nervous of the bouncers – that's what Clive called the two large men in dinner jackets and bow ties who were hovering negligently in the lobby.

I had time, while Clive was showing his tickets, to look round the small carpeted space, filled like a jungle with exotic green plants which fronded over the desk and curled round the backs of the armchairs.

When Clive took my coat from my shoulders I cringed.

Was it all right? I didn't want to look at his face, in case . . .

'You look marvellous!' he said.

There was no mistaking the admiration in his voice.

I dared to look round, and it was in his face as well. I smiled. I grinned. I was so happy. The dress was right – you could feel it, in that place already – I was with Clive and nothing else mattered.

And then I was completely disorientated. You had to get to the main part of the club through a bending corridor made, it seemed, of black mirror with lights on the floor. My vision was thrown completely off – I was wildly befuddled, and turned to Clive, my mouth open to protest.

'Fun, isn't it?' he said.

'No,' I said. 'It's horrible. What are they trying to do? Send you round the bend? No pun intended,' I added as the corridor took another alarming turn.

'Put you in the right mood, I think,' said Clive. And then, suddenly, we were in the middle of a mass of people.

I tried to say something, but there was too much noise. I was used to discos, but this was deafening. And I suppose, going through that corridor, you began to lose all sense of what was normal anyway.

I heard Clive mutter in my ear, but I couldn't hear. He laughed, and grabbed my arm, whisking me down three or four steps into the thick of the dancing people. It was like being in the middle of 'Top of the Pops', only miles better of course, with more fantastic lights bouncing off the walls and ceiling.

I felt wonderful, the silk of the skirt whirling round my legs and clinging to my hips the way you always dream of a dress doing. I wondered whether the neck was too low – but not for long. It seemed to stay where it was quite happily, however energetic I was on the dance floor.

Clive said something else, but this time I didn't even try to hear what he said. I just followed happily, back up the steps and into one of the far corners where there was a bar and comparatively less noise.

It was quite a struggle to get there, and when we did it looked as if there would be a very long wait before we could get served. The people waiting seemed to be about six deep. But there must have been plenty of people serving because it didn't, in fact, take very long. I asked for an orange juice and wondered, too late, if I was being unsophisticated. The trouble was, I didn't really know what to ask for. At home, if we had any alcohol around, I preferred beer. My parents are really quite good about that. They don't approve of me going into pubs, but they'll always let me have a drink at home when they've got some in.

'Nothing stronger?' His smile was amused, and I wasn't sure I liked that.

'I'm thirsty,' I said truthfully. It certainly wasn't the place where I could drink beer, not in this slinky dress especially.

'It's the thing at Jocasta's to have a cocktail,' he said. 'Some of them are a bit peculiar, but some are very nice.'

'I'll have whatever you recommend next time,' I said recklessly.

'After the next dance?'

'All right. Listen — your favourite record.'

'Come on,' he said, taking both our drinks and parking them before pulling me onto the dance floor again.

When it stopped he crushed me close and said right into my ear, 'How about having a go over there?'

He nodded his head towards the raised octagonal floor over at the far corner. It was more brilliantly lit, the focus of all the whirling lights. I'd noticed already that this was where all the really good dancers were, a kind of exhibition stage.

'But that's . . .' I thought perhaps I ought to tell him.

'I know.' His eyes were sparkling like the faceted mirror lights sweeping round overhead.

'But . . .' I didn't know what to say. My mind was a mixture of panic and wild confidence. 'But you're good!' I heard myself say stupidly.

He laughed, his white, even teeth like a film star's: he really was good-looking. 'So are you,' he said.

He'd convinced me.

I can't tell anyone how fantastic it felt to be on that floor. Even the computer which controlled the laser lights seemed to be on my side, picking up every movement as we did complicated whirls and turns, blending greens and reds over my head, funnelling solid cones of smoke round our feet.

Everything was perfect – up till then.

When we came down from the octagonal floor a couple hailed Clive, and he quickened his pace, following them towards the bar.

'Frankie, this is Len – we work together – and – Jennifer, is it?'

'Jennifer,' said Jennifer. 'Hello Frankie.'

'Nice to meet you,' said Len. 'Drinks?'

I opened my mouth to ask for an orange juice, but Clive interrupted. 'She's going to try one of Jocasta's famous cocktails, Len.'

'Fine. What colour do you fancy – blue, pink or white?' They laughed together and I felt they were mocking me for not knowing what the cocktails were.

'I'll have a blue one this time,' said Jennifer, hitching herself onto one of the bar stools and dangling her long elegant legs.

For the first time since that wonderful moment when Clive had breathed into my ear, 'You look marvellous' I felt awkward, gauche. I was sure my make-up had gone streaky with sweat after all that dancing, and I was conscious of damp patches on the flimsy fabric under my arms.

And Jennifer was beautiful. I mean, really beautiful. One of those kind of people who look like a model, all eyelashes and perfectly groomed hair, and the right kind of clothes. Her dress, in pale champagne, made mine look tarty and garish. Her pale hair seemed to match the material perfectly and I was all too conscious that my hair, brighter red in those glaring lights, clashed perhaps not as daringly as I'd thought, but only looked as if I had no sense of colour at all.

And then some more people came along who seemed to know Clive. There was a whirl of introductions and I didn't remember anyone's names any more. The blue drink, in a conical glass topped with palm trees and a Japanese parasol, spearing cherries and other fruit, tasted nicer than I thought it would. I sat sipping, listening to the babble of talk, trying to think up something witty to say but failing miserably.

We didn't dance again. And Clive seemed to have forgotten that we were going to have something to eat from the refreshment place on the other side of the room. In any case, I would have been too miserable to eat. All the girls his friends had brought with them seemed impossibly old. I thought somebody soon would be bound to notice I looked miles younger than anybody else, and would come and throw me out. They didn't, but I still felt too young against these people whose knowledge of the world outside school was so great.

I kept trying to think what my mother would say. She wouldn't be at a loss for words, I knew. But in spite of all my training since I was old enough to understand, somehow what my mother would have said had no relevance at all to what they were saying

72

now. It seemed a steady stream of jokes I often didn't get the point of and chat about their work.

True, Clive did keep turning round to present me with one of his devastating smiles, and to say, 'Are you quite happy?' I nodded, each time. I mean, what can you say? 'No, Clive, I'm terribly miserable, I want to go on dancing, I want you to myself, I want everything as it was before'?

No. I couldn't.

I suppose that showed my childishness. I'm sure any of these leggy girls leaning so negligently at the bar would have dragged their blokes onto the floor if they wanted to dance. One couple did — one of the ones whose names I'd forgotten. It gave me a very mild satisfaction to see that they weren't anywhere near as good as we were, and certainly wouldn't have dared to exhibit themselves on the octagonal floor.

I sipped my second drink — or was it my third? I tried a little hazily to remember what coloured liquids had been pressed into my hand. I thought alcohol was supposed to make it easier for people to talk. It wasn't working very well. Or perhaps it was, and I hadn't noticed. I found, to my surprise, that I was talking rather fast to Jennifer of the champagne dress and hair. I can't remember what we were talking about. At the time I thought it was a remarkably intelligent conversation.

Time passed by very quickly. I was astonished when Clive made movements to go. I thought he was getting up to dance, and rose with a brilliant smile. He took my arm, and instead of moving over to the dance floor he led me back through the winding tunnel where even the lights looked tired.

I stumbled a bit on that black, mirrored glass.

'Too many cocktails?' said Clive with amusement in his voice.

'Not at all,' I assured him. 'It's this tunnel again. Makes you feel peculiar.'

When we got outside the cold air hit me, and I realised that it was not just the tunnel making me feel peculiar.

How many cocktails had I had, for goodness' sake?

'Careful!' protested Clive as I lurched towards him on the way to the car park.

'Sorry. Bump in the pavement,' I apologised. I clung to his arm and felt him pull me tighter towards him.

'Just hang on to me,' he said.

I was only too glad. I didn't think I'd make it on my own. But that wasn't the only thing. If I'd been only wobbly on my feet I wouldn't have minded at all. Clive seemed perfectly prepared to stop me falling over, and it was rather nice to be cuddled against him, even if I did feel a bit stupid, lurching over the uneven ground of the car park. There were probably plenty of others doing the same thing.

The truth was, I felt sick.

There's nothing more calculated to ruin a nice romantic evening than wanting to be sick, and trying very hard to keep control of your stomach, especially in a rather bumpy car which, though I'd only noticed it this moment, smelled of leaky petrol and damp.

I managed to give Clive a wan smile as we stopped at a traffic light, and he put his arm protectively around me. I remember thinking vaguely that he shouldn't be doing that, that you ought to have both hands on the steering wheel, then it all became too much effort and I let my face drop into the scratchy wool of his sleeve. It smelled a lot nicer than the car – faintly masculine, with a touch of after-shave, I thought, and that nice clean fabric smell as well. It seemed to stave off the sick feeling, besides being extremely comfortable.

I think I dozed a little, because the next thing I knew the lights of town had disappeared. The car was slowing down, and he gently disentangled my head from his arm to move the gear lever.

'What?' I said drowsily.

For answer he turned in the driving seat, put both arms round me and began searching for my mouth. My stomach protested. I couldn't – I really couldn't.

I pushed at him, but he seemed to think I was being coy or something, because he only grabbed me tighter.

'Clive!' when I got my mouth free. 'Want – be *sick*!'

I don't know how I got the car door open. I don't know whether he was helping or if he hadn't understood and was trying to stop me. I did, however, get it open in time.

I stood on the grass verge in the middle of nowhere, retching and crying and wishing I'd never been born.

At last it was all over. I stood shivering, ashamed and furious at myself. If I'd known where I was I'd have run home. I almost did anyway. I just wanted to disappear, it didn't matter where to.

But he was really sweet.

'All right now?' he said. His voice was gentle, really kind.

'I think so. Sorry.'

'My fault for stuffing you with cocktails when you weren't used to them. I should have insisted you stayed on the same one anyway. It's mixing them too much. You'll have quite a headache tomorrow.'

'I won't. It's gone already,' I assured him.

'Well, that's all right, then,' he said easily. 'Now if you think you can bear it, get back in and I'll drive you home as quickly as possible.'

'Not too quick,' I whispered, getting in again, 'just in case. Are you very angry?'

'I might have been if you'd been sick in my car,' he said. I didn't know whether he was teasing or not. I couldn't look at him. I was sure he was disgusted with me.

We drew up outside my house. I looked up at the windows. No lights, but you couldn't tell, as my parents sleep at the back of the house.

'Is it this one? It's all right, Cinderella. I won't come in to meet the wicked stepmother. I'll just wait till you're inside.'

How did he know about my mother? my brain asked somewhere at the back of my head. But I was too muddled and ashamed of myself to think any more.

He didn't kiss me. I wouldn't have wanted to kiss someone who had just been sick either. I walked unsteadily up the path, found my key, and found, slightly surprisingly, the lock. As the door opened I heard him let in the clutch – a knock as if a kilo weight was dropping into a large, empty metal can. It was enormously loud in the still night.

I turned, waved, and went in. I don't know whether he waved back.

Chapter 7

It was so different from last time. Then I had been half happy, because of the wonderful evening at the party, half miserable because I didn't know whether he would phone me again. This time I was totally miserable. It hadn't been as wonderful as I'd thought at Jocasta's — that is, the first half of it had been magic, but when his friends had come along I just knew I wasn't old enough. I didn't even hope he would call. After the exhibition I'd made of myself I knew he wouldn't.

I didn't surprise my parents by getting up early. I didn't want to see them or talk to them. I just lay in my bed and felt ill.

I suppose most of it was a hangover. I was terribly thirsty and still a bit sick. I wanted to sleep for ever. I didn't want to think at all. It was too painful. But somehow I couldn't sleep properly, only dozed and felt hot and uncomfortable.

I dragged myself out of bed at about midday. A bath made me feel much better, but then when I went back into my room I saw the red dress, dropped in a heap on the floor, reminding me only too forcibly of last night.

I picked the thing up and pushed it to the back of a drawer. It would have to be washed, or cleaned, sometime, but that could wait till I felt unconcerned enough to see it again. Perhaps in about twenty years, when I was older, I could pull it out and think, 'Ah, that was the time when I was young and silly. I'm glad I never did anything as stupid as that again.'

I suppose you've got to learn by your mistakes, but it seems a very painful way of getting educated.

The next thing was to face my parents.

I just didn't know what they were going to say. I knew they'd been awake when I got home because the light from their bedroom didn't quite go off in time before I came through the front door.

They were really sweet, though. They behaved as if nothing different had happened at all.

'Afternoon,' said my father when I went into the dining room. They were both sitting over bowls of soup, reading the Sunday papers. 'Would you prefer breakfast, lunch or dinner?'

I saw my mother's mouth open and then shut again as she caught Dad's eye.

'Juice?' she said brightly.

I suppose she knew about my raging thirst, but I was grateful that that was her only comment, ever.

I sat down with them and poured what seemed like a reservoir of juice, coffee, water, anything liquid down my throat, and felt a great deal better. And still they didn't say anything.

When the telephone rang it didn't occur to me to answer it, so I was doubly surprised when Dad came back and said, 'It's for you.'

Even then I didn't think.

'Me? Who?' I'd expected Sonia, or Caz perhaps. Even Alan.

'I don't know,' he said. 'Some gentleman.'

I couldn't believe it. It was Clive. I really didn't believe it. Not until he actually spoke at the other end of the line.

'Cinderella? How are you?'

'Clive!' I squeaked into the receiver. 'How did you . . . ?'

'An enormous amount of detective work,' he assured me solemnly. 'You told me your surname, remember? For an intelligent chap like me it's just routine to look in the directory, match up the name with the address and memorise the number.'

I felt just enough self-possession to say shakily, 'Well done, Holmes.'

'And how are you?' he persisted. 'Recovered?'

'All right, thanks. Clive, I'm really sorry about that . . .'

'Think nothing of it,' he said easily. 'Happens to all of us at some time. I was wondering, if you felt strong enough, if you'd like to come for a healthy walk over the fields, blow the cobwebs away, just for an hour.'

Would I? From feeling so down that I might have been sitting at the bottom of a mine shaft, I felt as if I was flying over the top of Everest.

'Love to,' I said coolly. 'I'll meet you . . .'

'I know, on the corner.' I could hear the teasing in his voice. 'In half an hour?'

'Make it three-quarters,' I said, and put the phone down in a daze.

'Alan?' queried my mother when I went back to finish my cooling soup.

'A friend of his,' I said, not meeting her eyes. 'We're going for a walk this afternoon. All of us.'

And I rubbed my eyes as if with sleep, so that she couldn't see the lie in them.

'Do you good, I should think,' said my father. 'I'd come with you only I said I'd go over to Harman

Hall for the Sunday market with your mother later on.'

I didn't know whether he was being serious. I decided to treat it as a joke.

'What a pity,' I said casually. 'I'd like to see you sloshing about in ditches.'

'More likely than seeing you,' he said tartly, and quite truthfully.

'Well, I'll go and get ready then,' I said. It seemed a good idea to get out of the way before I got asked any more questions I didn't want to answer. 'I'll wash up after dinner, if that's all right?'

It was my usual job to wash up after lunch at weekends.

'Suits me,' said my mother. 'I'd much rather do these. Have a nice walk. See you later.'

The scent of damp earth and the tracery of winter branches seemed like something just thought of, a new creation, and yet I don't remember very much about that walk. There was the feel of Clive's arm, in a lined anorak, rough and bulky. There was the sound of his voice, saying what seemed to be profound statements about life, but again I didn't remember anything about it afterwards. I was just happy. He could have been reciting valency tables for all I knew: it still would have sounded profound.

As my father had predicted, we didn't slosh about in ditches. Clive was much too careful of his shoes for that. My mother, of course, would have called him fussy, and laughed at anyone wearing clean polished shoes on a country walk. She and Dad would have put on Wellingtons and really sloshed about in ditches. They'd be all understanding about the world and talk about how they would conserve it and join societies to do so, which of course they have. And Alan too, which is probably another reason why they get on so well.

I was thinking about all this later in the evening, in the middle of lovely dreams of Clive. So I don't know why that sudden thought of Alan gave me such a pang. I suppose I missed his conversation. You do miss people when you've known them all your life and suddenly they disappear out of it.

Still, I suppose he was busy with that girl Julie. Good luck to him. Thank goodness I'd got Clive, or I might, I thought, have been jealous.

It was awful having to go to school next day – not because I was worried about Clive not ringing now, but because it was the week before our mock O levels, and I knew I hadn't done enough work. Even Clive had said so – though he'd been really nice about it. Of course, what I wanted him to say was, 'I've got to see you every day, even if you have got exams coming up,' but I knew that wouldn't have been very sensible. And of course he didn't. I think I said something grumpy like, 'Oh, hell, we've got our mocks next week,' because he was instantly sympathetic.

'Look,' he said, before he left me at the corner, 'you've got to work hard. Make me proud of you. I'm not going to see you till Saturday – all right? We'll go to a film. Do you like space films? There's a good one on at the Odeon – had great reviews.'

I'd have watched the nastiest B movie, anywhere, if it was with Clive.

'It sounds great,' I said. I wasn't really disappointed. I knew, this time, I was going to go out with him soon. I hoped I'd be able to work, if I'd got Saturday to look forward to. I just knew I'd spend all my waking hours thinking about him, reliving the delicate touch of his hand on mine, the time he'd said I looked marvellous, trying, probably, to push away the memory of those terribly assured friends of his, and the cocktails . . . I was sure even the sight of a Japanese paper parasol would make me feel sick for the rest of my life.

And I'd really *have* to work. I'd left it for so long. I'd work for him, really make him proud of me.

And then, when it was all over, there would be our fifth year Christmas disco. I'd ask him to come with me. It would be marvellous to have him as a partner, showing up everyone else's boyfriends. He would be the best looking boy there. All the other blokes I knew were pimply and gawky. Wouldn't they all be envious! I just hoped Sonia would still be speaking, and wouldn't be embarrassed if I brought him along. Even if we had been a bit off each other lately, I didn't really want to upset her. When we were friends we got on really well.

But I had another surprise on Monday.

Sonia actually spoke to me. She came up and talked as if nothing had happened these last weeks. We were back to being friends again. You don't know how much nicer it was being at school. I suppose you don't realise how miserable you've been until it stops. Everything, suddenly, was wonderful. And Sonia was all sparkle-eyed as well. It didn't take me long to find out: she was going out with John!

I did think she might have told me. After all, there I was, trying to get her interested in my love life, and all the time she was sneaking off to the cinema with him.

'I wasn't sure,' confessed Sonia at dinner break. She'd come round the back of the biology lab — our favourite place for a gossip, where not many people went because it was a bit draughty — and left poor old John practising football for a match next Saturday. 'He asked me out, but he didn't ask again, and . . .'

It was all very familiar.

We had a marvellous gossip, and compared notes, and suddenly I felt as if life had meaning again, except, of course, for those looming exams next week. However, I could even put up with them if Clive said he'd come to the Christmas disco with me.

I wouldn't be able to buy anything new to wear. That red dress, still at the back of my drawer, haunted me. I began to tell Sonia about it once, but I felt so silly that I didn't. Then I had to think about my mother's birthday present. It was right in the middle of those exams, so I'd arranged to go into town with Sonia the Saturday before to buy something for her — the Saturday I was to go to the film with Clive.

'I thought you were going to get her that sandwich toaster?' said Sonia on Friday.

'Well, the thing is . . .' and it all came out.

She's a nice friend to have, Sonia, even if she does go on a bit about my mother sometimes. She was so understanding about that dress.

'Why didn't you ask me to come with you?' she

said. 'I'd have made sure you didn't get anything too expensive.'

'You?' I said. 'I'd have asked you any time, but you weren't speaking to me then.'

It was the only time I ever said anything about those last few weeks, and she took it as a joke, really nicely.

'Couldn't get a word in edgeways,' she said, mock grumbling. And that was the very last of the nastiness gone. 'Let's have a look at it some time.'

'It's all right, I suppose.' I said. 'Red. Silky. All tight round the top and swoopy round the bottom. Lovely to dance in.'

Sonia said she was madly envious, and it was probably worth not being able to get my mother's sandwich toaster this time. 'You've got to spend a lot on a thing like that,' she said reassuringly. 'Anything cheap would look cheap.'

'I suppose you're right,' I said gratefully. 'But what about my mother's present? I've hardly got anything left.'

We discussed all the things she'd like, then Sonia remembered about this book she wanted.

'You know, Alan said she ought to read it. But it was ages ago. She might have read it by now.'

'No, she hasn't. If she had she and Alan would have been talking about it non-stop, and I'd have had to read it too.'

Then I stopped. Of course, Alan hadn't been round for a long time. It seemed strange. I don't think he'd ever been away from our house that long before, except when he went on holiday. Suddenly, now that I thought about it, I missed his company, missed the energetic exchange of ideas that had been so much a part of my life.

But I didn't let Sonia see this. I went on hurriedly, 'There's no way you can forget anything my mother's read if it's as special as all that. And it's in paperback – no problem about the money, then.'

'And this time *you* can come with *me* and choose something for me to dazzle John in at the disco.'

We did. It was lovely, and somehow made Sonia's curves look a pleasing plump instead of bulging in the wrong places like she often did when she didn't bother too much. It seems awful talking like this about your best friend, but she's just as rude to me about my mother so I've got to get a bit of my own back sometimes. I had a sneaky look round for something I'd have been able to get if I hadn't squandered everything on my red dress, but fortunately there was nothing I really liked or I'd have been feeling sick with envy.

I would just have to wear the green one again. Anyway, he said he liked it, even that very first time we went out together. I could do my hair differently, so that he could comment on that instead of my dress.

'Will you do my hair that afternoon, Sonia?' I asked after we'd been to the bookshop and found my mother's birthday book, which cost all I had left except the bus fare home.

'Me?'

'Yes – you know, make it look really way out.'

She looked doubtfully at me. 'I can do my own, but I don't know if . . .'

'Don't be silly,' I said impatiently, 'if you can do

yours, you can do mine. It's much easier doing someone else's.'

'So long as you do mine, then,' she said.

'Better start early,' I grinned, 'then if I make a mess of it we'll have plenty of time to do it all again!'

That was the last day of fun for another week. We were plunged into the rest of the exams. I felt like a zombie by Friday lunch-time, when it had all ended.

'Let's go into town, Sonia. I need a gallon of coffee to wake me up,' I groaned.

'Sorry. Going already with John,' she said.

It's funny how quickly your mood can change. I'd been fairly happy with those exams – some had been awful, some quite good, but I didn't feel as if I was going to fail absolutely everything. And the last one had been art: quite soothing, really. While I was happily sloshing paint about, I thought of Clive, and of his arm round me in the cinema last week, and what we might do tonight, and how I'd ask him to the disco. Then I thought the best thing to do after a load of exams is just flop in a café in town.

And she'd let me down.

It was silly, of course. Just because John is in our form anyway, I ought to have realised she'd rather go with him.

I did try not to show how let down I felt. I just laughed and said all right then, Caz and Jane and I would follow them and see that they weren't kissing in corners. But then Caz and Jane said they were doing something different as well. Everybody had their own ideas of what they were going to do.

I didn't wait for school lunch. I put on my coat and scarf and went out into the driving rain, walking fast because I didn't want to stop, even though a bus was coming in the distance.

Then I changed my mind. There'd be no point going into town by myself. I didn't want to sit and drink coffee on my own. I hadn't enough money to do anything else.

I found myself walking, almost blindly, to the side of town where Alan lived. I'd never gone there as often as Alan had come to us, but I still knew my way automatically. The rain soaked into my hair and made the scarf round my neck a cold misery.

I'd forgotten both his parents would be at work. I'd forgotten he'd probably be at college. But fortunately for me he was at home. If he hadn't been I think I'd have curled up in the front garden under the leafless roses and cried.

I told him about it when I'd got dried and warm and had boiling instant coffee handed to me in a familiar mug.

'And they'd have taken you away in a plain van,' Alan said solemnly. 'Of course, they'd realise it was only the shock of exams. You'd have been let out within three months.'

He didn't say anything silly like, 'Fancy seeing you after all this time,' or anything like that. It was quite natural that I should be there, and even more natural that I should have gone there because I was upset at having nobody to let off steam with after exams were over.

We seemed to pick up our friendship from where we left off, weeks ago. It wasn't till I said I'd better get off home, or Mum might think I'd done so badly in maths I'd drowned myself, that he said anything that even acknowledged his long separation from us.

'I must come and see your mother some time soon,' he said. 'I seem to have been pretty busy lately.'

'Julie?' I said, trying to find a dry bit of scarf, failing, and stuffing it like a drowned woolly caterpillar into the top of my bag.

'That – and other things,' he said.

I waved goodbye cheerily and said, 'See you soon,' and things like that.

But as I went down the road I had a strange feeling of loss.

Chapter 8

At least I didn't have to lie to my mother about where I was going this time. Even though I wasn't going to tell her who I was going with. It was easy: I said I was going over to Sonia's for the afternoon so that we could do each other's hair, then we were going to have tea there, and go out to the disco afterwards.

This seemed quite reasonable to my mother. We'd often done that, perhaps going out to the afternoon film, coming back and playing with make-up or trying on each other's clothes. Not that there was much of mine that Sonia could get into nowadays, but we both took the same size shoes and she always buys really fantastic, fashionable ones. I think her clothes allowance is a bit more than mine. It must be. Shoes are so expensive.

'I suppose you're asking Alan?' she said.

'Honestly, Mum, I don't have Alan on a string!' I said. 'In any case, he's got a girlfriend at college.'

That made her think. She'd been so sure that we had been destined for each other from the cradle that I don't think it had ever occurred to her that either of us might prefer somebody else.

In fact she looked almost bewildered – not at all my capable, argumentative, thinking-things-out mother – so much that *I* began to feel sorry for *her*.

'Have you got anyone to go with?' she said, sort of trying to seem unconcerned.

'Oh, there are plenty of people to ask. Even if there weren't, there'll be lots of spare blokes in our year.'

'Yes, but . . .'

'And I'm going with Sonia,' I reminded her, as if we were going together. I hadn't told her about Sonia and John.

'I suppose you'll be all right, then,' she said doubtfully.

'Oh, Mum, stop worrying about me,' I said impatiently. If she went on any more I'd think I really didn't have anyone to go with and start crying. As it was I went up to my room and first giggled, then felt guilty I couldn't tell her about Clive.

It was a pity really. I'd have liked to bring someone home, in the easy way Alan came, but it could never be the same as that. I wasn't sure how Mum would react to someone like Clive, and I didn't want to risk it. So far, anyway, he was quite happy at leaving me on the corner of the street. It seemed to amuse him.

And he hadn't seemed to mind at all about that

night at Jocasta's. When we went to the cinema, the Saturday before exams, he had held my hand in the nicest way. And when the story got emotional, when the ship looked as if it was doomed and I wanted to hide because my eyes had started to drip, his arm had come creeping round my shoulder and a clean white hankie was pressed into my hand. There hadn't been any problem about coming home, because he'd had to go straight on somewhere after the film, so he just took me to the bus stop and gave me a kiss when it came.

It's really lovely being treated the way Clive treats me, as if I was the only person in the world who mattered. I didn't want to share him with anyone, especially my family. They'd take over and he'd turn into another person, or, which I knew was more likely, get put off completely.

And now that the mocks were over I could spend all my time thinking about him and about what I would wear for the Christmas disco. Sonia had suggested putting a dark blue belt on my green dress and wearing dark blue tights and the really long dangly earrings we'd bought on a shopping expedition so long ago I'd forgotten about them. At first, I said you couldn't put a belt on that dress because the gathers would bulge. But she was right, and the whole outfit looked really fantastic. I liked it even better than my red slinky (which was how I thought of it now) and I knew I felt comfortable in it.

But just now I had to stop thinking about the dance and worry about what I was going to wear to the cinema this evening. Somehow the thought of sitting holding hands in the cinema in the evening, rather than the afternoon, sent shivers down my spine. And there was something quite different about coming home late with him than coming home, tamely, to supper.

I agonised for ages over what to wear. I kept trying things on and taking them off again till my room looked like a jumble sale. In the end I settled for my jeans and a dolman sleeved jumper, which I love but which always seems a bit too dressy for hanging about the house in or even going round town in.

'You look very nice,' said my mother at tea time. I'd asked if we could eat early so that I could get the bus at six. I wasn't getting a bus at all, but Clive said we could have a drive round first before going to the film at eight.

'Thanks,' I said, casually I hoped.

'You don't usually dress up as much as that for the pictures, do you?' she said. It's relentless, the way my mother won't leave the subject alone.

'No,' I said, 'but there's always a first time.'

'Are you seeing anyone special?'

'*No!*' I said. 'I've got to wear it some time, haven't I, before I grow out of it? Why not now?'

'Why not,' agreed my mother. She didn't go on any more, thank goodness, but it had made me so nervy that at six I rushed out of the house yelling, 'Cheerio! See you later,' and slammed the door behind me in a way which I hoped would make it quite clear I didn't want any more nosing about what I was doing.

He wasn't on the corner.

My heart stopped for a moment.

Was he going to come at all?

It's silly, I know, to think someone's let you down when he's not there to meet you. Especially when I was, in fact, early. But I was still twitching about my parents coming to see whether I was really at the bus stop, which I wasn't. The bus is over the road and round the corner in the other direction. I was scared even to look back towards our house in case they were watching out of a window.

And then, the relief, he arrived, the little green MG roaring down the road and pulling up with a squeal of brakes which wouldn't have shamed a lorry.

'What a row!' I said. 'All the neighbours will rush to their net curtains to see what's going on.'

'Good thing too,' he grinned, taking off again with a scream of tyres that can't have done them any good. (I was beginning to think like Dad now – honestly, all this thinking seriously about life can dampen your excitement!) 'It's time your wicked stepmother knew about the Prince Charming in the background.'

It made our relationship seem so permanent, the way he said things. I saved that one up to tell Sonia on Monday morning. I bet John never said wonderfully romantic things like that to her. Knowing John, I'm one hundred per cent certain he wouldn't know how to, even if he thought them.

I've got to be honest at this point, and you'll probably think I was really stupid.

I didn't know how to ask him to the disco.

It's all very well saying women are equal and all that, but when it comes to asking people out it's usually the bloke that does it. We were right back to square one. Alan I could have asked as easily as anything, but then he was my friend. I suppose I could have asked anyone else from school who'd left. I just didn't have the faintest idea how to start asking Clive.

I didn't enjoy the film one bit, I was thinking about it all the time. Then when we came out and he said, 'Well?' I didn't know what he was talking about.

'Well?' I repeated stupidly.

'What did you think of it?'

'Oh – I – er – it was great.'

'What's on your mind, Frankie?'

I felt warm and wanted again. He cared enough about me to know something was bothering me. Feeling quite ridiculous, and stammering like a baby, I said, 'It's the school dance. I wondered – if you'd come with me.'

I'd said it. It was out. The relief was immense. I hardly heard his reply.

'School dance? Not my sort of thing, really. I can't see me prancing about with a lot of school kids.'

I don't ever remember being so shatteringly, desperately humiliated. My face burned and I walked quickly into the dark shadows of the car park so that he couldn't see.

'Well, it was only an idea,' I said, I hoped lightly. 'A bit much for your sophistication, I suppose.'

For answer he opened the car doors quickly, leaned across from the driving seat and as soon as I was in he started kissing me in the darkness – until someone switched on his headlights which blazed right through the MG's windscreen and with a laugh he pulled himself away.

It was lovely, and thrilling, but underneath I had a hard lump in my chest, a sick kind of disappointment which wouldn't go away even when he was whispering wonderful complimentary things in between kisses on the corner where he always left me.

'I've got to go,' I said thickly between kisses.

'All right, Cinderella. Next Saturday?'

'That's the dance,' I said flatly.

'Friday, then.' It didn't seem to matter. I said yes that would be lovely, gave him a quick peck on the cheek, then lurched out of the car before my eyes filled too suspiciously with tears.

I didn't know how to face Sonia on Monday. In the end I just didn't say anything at all. I threw myself into end of term events with an enthusiasm which startled the teachers and even made my mother comment how unlike me it was. She was convinced I was going out with someone at school and that was why I wanted to stay behind to help with so many things. I even volunteered to bake three dozen savouries for the dance on Saturday – *me*, voluntarily cooking! And after I'd said it, I didn't know when I was going to do it, since I was going out with Clive on Friday night. At least I didn't have to lie about that to Sonia as well as everyone else. I can't even remember what excuse I gave my mother for having to go out on Friday night instead of making those savoury things. I said tetchily I'd do them in the morning, no problem, and that I was not going over to Sonia's till about two, so even if I didn't get up very early I'd still have plenty of time.

'Yes, but what about me wanting to use the kitchen?' asked my mother. 'How do you expect me to plan my own day if I don't know when you're going to be puddling about?'

'What a cheek, puddling about!' I said, still determinedly cheerful. I don't know how I managed to keep my tears so well buried. I kept feeling them building up from a sort of frozen block inside me somewhere, as if when the pressure was lifted they'd come bursting out like a geyser. 'All right, I'll start doing them at eleven, then I'll be out of the way all afternoon. Okay?'

'If you want any help . . .' offered my mother.

'I'm better at these things,' said my father. 'Come on, now, admit it. You're marvellous at spaghetti bolognese and bread and exotic salads, but when it comes to pastry things I'm the chef you need.'

'Pastrycook,' she corrected automatically. But she was quite relieved all the same. She hates making pastry. Actually, so do I, so I was quite glad of Dad's offer. I accepted, and made sure I'd bought everything I needed before Friday night.

I tried not to think that there was just nobody for me to ask. Even if it wasn't so late by now there wouldn't have been anyone. I mean, I'd gone around a lot with John – not as a boyfriend, but just in the gang, as a friend. It was always me who did daft things, like having that ride on his bike before he passed his test. There were other boys I knew on the same friendly footing.

I couldn't, of course, ask Alan.

Everyone else seemed to be paired off in our old gang now. Caz and Jane had been giggling in corners about their boyfriends – sixth formers from another school at our end of town. And there was no one else around that I fancied asking, even if they weren't going to be there anyway. Our own sixth year seemed always too remote and toffee-nosed even to speak to us lot, let alone be interested in coming to our disco.

'You're very quiet tonight,' teased Clive.

We were going to have our usual drive into the country before going to the cinema. For some reason there was a spate of good films at that time, and I was enjoying those evenings in the half-empty place, cuddling up to him in the darkness. The Western we saw last week, particularly, was much better on the big screen. Cowboys don't seem to swagger quite as convincingly on television.

'Am I?' I said.

'Where shall we go now? It's a bit dark to see anything much. Want a quick drink at the pub before we go to the film?'

'Why not?' I said.

He didn't ask what I wanted – just bought an orange juice, for which I was grateful. Though in a way I felt slightly annoyed he didn't ask me.

I tried to stop myself feeling bitter. I was having a wonderful evening now, wasn't I? Sitting in the warmth of the pub, the cold of the December night closed off by thick red curtains, the brass gleaming, the voices, so early, still quiet. The fact that I was going to be by myself tomorrow had nothing to do with now.

I couldn't not go. Not after saying to my mother so confidently that I was going. And I didn't know how Sonia would react, when she saw Clive hadn't come. I didn't know if she'd be sympathetic or nasty. I think I would almost prefer her to be nasty.

At least I wouldn't have to put up with my mother

being sympathetic, asking what had gone wrong and analysing the situation.

'You really are quiet tonight,' said Clive. 'Is there something wrong?'

'No,' I said. 'Should there be?'

'You're usually so bubbly. If I didn't know better I'd think you were a different person. You haven't got a twin, have you?' in mock alarm.

I laughed.

'That's better,' he said. 'Now come and tell Uncle Clive all about it.' He sat closer to me on the oak settle and patted my hand.

I took a *very* deep breath. Isn't it awful when tears keep threatening to come pouring out of your eyes just at the moment you want to be at your most cool?

'There's nothing to tell,' I said. It came out a bit stiffly, but I didn't cry.

'Of course there is,' he pressed. 'Now come on, or I shan't take you to the movie.'

'Honestly, Clive, there isn't anything.'

'All right, there isn't anything wrong. Absolutely nothing at all. So if there isn't anything wrong, you can tell me why you're not your usual self tonight. Is it something I've done?'

'No!' I said, too violently.

'Then it must be something I haven't done,' he went on inexorably. 'Come on, Frankie. How have I upset you?'

'Oh, nothing,' I said lamely. 'Stop making a great big issue of it. It doesn't matter at all, honestly. I was just a bit disappointed that you couldn't make it to the dance tomorrow, and I was wondering what it was going to be like on my own, that's all.'

I'd said it now. This was probably the end. I looked round for my gloves. I was so sure he'd be annoyed and want to go.

'Is that all? In that case, Cinderella, I'd love to take you to the ball. I can't have you upsetting yourself. I'm sure I'll manage to behave properly. I thought you'd have strings of admirers ready to step into the breach. You should have told me how important it was.'

'Oh, it's not as important as all that . . .' I began, and stopped myself. How did you tell him how important it was without him feeling trapped? So I just shut up and grinned at him.

'There you are. I told you there was something wrong,' he said. 'Now finish up your orange juice like a good girl and we'll go and see that film before it's too late.'

If I felt the tiniest bit uncomfortable at his indulgent tone I ignored it. How glad I was I hadn't said anything to my parents! I was even more glad I hadn't said anything to Sonia. I just hoped she wasn't going to be embarrassed. No, she probably wouldn't be now. I just hoped, then, that *Clive* wouldn't be embarrassed at being confronted with Sonia.

No, I didn't care about any of these things. He was coming to the Christmas disco with me.

I was on cloud nine.

Chapter 9

I got up early as I'd said I would to make the savouries, and my parents swopped their mornings for lying in bed so Dad and I had an unaccustomed breakfast together. I must say it's quite nice having him to myself at breakfast. We sat companionably, eating boiled eggs and toast, me getting stuck into one of those library books that you can't put down, Dad with the paper spread all over the milk jug, the toast rack and the marmalade. It was all thoroughly scruffy and we didn't talk at all.

We spent at least three-quarters of an hour in this lovely mess, but then the time came when we had to get going on the pastry.

'I'll wash up,' I said. 'You get the pastry things ready. You wouldn't like to make the whole thing yourself?' I was hopeful.

'No. You volunteered, you do it. I'm just going to stand by and give a bit of fatherly advice from time to time.'

'Oh, big deal!'

I was still in my dressing gown, and by the time I'd splashed washing up water all over it and spilt flour down the front, I was in a thoroughly nasty mood. The calm of that early breakfast had gone.

'Why don't you go and get dressed,' suggested Dad.

'I suppose you think it's wrong to make pastry with a dressing gown on?' I sneered.

'I think you'd find it more comfortable,' he said mildly.

'Oh, you — you want to do everything the proper

way!'

'I only suggested . . .'

But I didn't want to hear any more. I slammed upstairs, banging doors and making a huge fuss.

I don't know why I was so nervous. I ought to have been so happy, with Clive coming to the disco tonight. I suppose it was because he'd said so definitely that it wasn't his sort of thing. I felt as if I'd bullied him into going, and that he'd hate it. It would be childish, compared to the places he'd taken me.

I'd better get on with my cooking. Sonia could help me take them up to school this afternoon. Apart from the fact they wanted the food early to set it out, I didn't think the sight of me with trays of pastry things would make him any more enthusiastic.

When I came down again, comfortable in my old jeans and sweater and Dad's big butcher's apron wrapped round me, my mother had got up.

It was disastrous.

She didn't interfere with our cooking. She just sat eating wholemeal toast and nagging on about Alan. She was so sure that I was going with him, even though I'd told her he'd got a girlfriend, that she couldn't keep off asking why he wasn't coming round. I couldn't concentrate on making the pastry. After putting too much water in one lot, so that we had to throw in more flour and unbalance the mixture of flour and fat, Dad said, 'Oh, let's start again.'

'We *can't*!' I almost screamed. 'There isn't enough flour, and in any case I don't want to be doing this all *day*!'

'I'll go out and get some, shall I?' offered my

mother, all understanding. 'Don't worry about it. We can always use up your failed pastry later on.'

'But it's *white* flour,' I wailed. She'd gone to all the trouble of buying white flour instead of the wholemeal she usually uses because I said we couldn't possibly have that hard stuff for a *party*, for goodness sake. But for our family it would be a waste and . . .

'It doesn't matter,' she reassured me. 'I don't see why we shouldn't have some party stuff as well. An hour or two in the fridge and we can use yours up quite easily.' And she was out of the door before I could protest any more.

So I now felt guilty as well as irritable.

If only he'd said he would come to the disco in the first place, then I wouldn't have felt like this. I began to wish I'd never nagged at him to come at all. If it had been Alan, he'd have come and helped me make the darned things and we could have had a great time even if we had made mistakes with the amount of water.

But it wasn't Alan, it was Clive, and I needed to impress him with my brilliance.

'Have a cup of tea,' joked my father. 'Sit down and collect yourself, as my mother used to say when I got into a flap about things.'

'You?' It hadn't occurred to me that my calm father ever got into a flap about things. Mum, yes, but Dad . . .

'All the time,' he said cheerfully. 'Put the kettle on while I wrap this lot up. An hour in the fridge will make it easy to work with, and we can start yours as soon as Mum gets back.'

I calmed down, and even listened to Mum rattling

on when she returned. Then my father gently but firmly pushed her into the sitting room with the paper and a record and told her to stay there until we'd finished.

They turned out really rather well, though I say it myself. We had lots of tiny things like cornish pasties, only inside we made sort of curry mixtures with meat, meat and vegetables and just vegetables. Then he invented something with baked beans and chilli powder to put in cases like Christmas mince pies.

'You're very good at this,' I said. 'Why haven't you made anything at home like them?'

'We don't have those sort of parties any more, I suppose,' he said. 'When we have friends in now it's more likely to be huge pots of chilli con carne. This stuff is cheating.'

'Nice, though,' I said greedily, scraping the pan.

They all turned out absolutely marvellously, and Dad promised to make something just as good for him and Mum that evening with the failed batch. 'It'll be a change to have something non-organic and thoroughly fattening,' he joked. 'Won't do us any harm just for once.'

Well, it may be much better for us to live on wholemeal things, but the party food looked and smelled and tasted delicious. I had quite cheered up by the time I was ready with them all carefully wrapped in napkins and gently placed in labelled polythene boxes.

'You look as if you're going away for a week,' said my mother, coming to the front door as I shouted goodbye. 'Ask Sonia round here next time. We can give her tea and you can change upstairs.'

She sounded almost sad. I suppose she missed having Alan's company. I must say he did used to liven the place up.

'Good idea,' I said. 'Get Dad to make some fancy thing for our tea then. Not,' I said hastily, 'that I mind what we usually have. It's just nice to have a change.'

'Oh, go away and enjoy yourself!' said my mother, laughing.

I found Sonia almost as nervous as myself. I suppose it was the first time she and John would be on public display, so to speak, because at school they don't even hold hands when anyone's looking. If you didn't know, you wouldn't suspect they were going out together.

'What time is he coming?' she fretted. 'John's coming at eight.'

I thanked my stars that I had managed to persuade him to come. Suppose I had to confess, now, that I would be going by myself.

I think by now I'd probably have caught something very infectious, and have had to stay at home.

'Clive's coming at eight as well,' I said, and watched closely for any reaction to his name. But she didn't seem at all concerned about him any more. Her mind was completely taken up by John. 'You're not going on the motorbike, are you?' I said.

'How else?'

'But your dress . . .'

'No problem,' she said. 'It's uncrushable. I've tried. I'll put these waterproof trousers over the top, and he's lent me a leather jacket, and we'll carry my shoes. The only thing that's worrying me is my hair. Can you think of a style that won't get completely squashed under a helmet?'

'No,' I said, 'to be honest. But we'll have a try. Shall we go up to school and deliver my food now, then we'll have the rest of the afternoon for experiments.'

'Let's have a look,' she said, always greedy about food. 'Can I try one?'

'One,' I said. 'Positively no more. I didn't spend all morning on them for you to hog the lot. What flavour?'

She was flatteringly enthusiastic, and we quickly wrapped them all up again before either of us became too tempted. We bussed to school and back, then returned to the serious business of hair.

Halfway through the afternnon I stopped, exasperated. 'Look, couldn't you come in Clive's car with us? Leave the motorbike behind and collect it when we come back?'

'No,' said Sonia. I knew how she felt.

I was quite relieved, really. I didn't want to share Clive's little car with anyone – even if they'd managed to squeeze into the tiny seats in the back – especially on the way home.

'You'll just have to put up with squashed hair then,' I said.

'I don't mind,' said Sonia. 'It'll go mad, dancing, anyway.'

'True,' I agreed.

I was quite pleased with my combination of dark blue and green, and when Sonia had finished with my hair it looked really great – better than I'd ever managed to do it before. And it was only just done in time before the bell rang.

We both shrieked in panic.

'I'm nowhere *near* ready!' said Sonia. 'You open the door — I want John to see me uncrushed and unsquashed and right even if it's only for five minutes.'

But it wasn't John. For a second I was struck dumb. Clive looked really cool — smart and yet not overdressed for a school disco. Compared to John, puffing up the path in his motorbike gear, he was fantastic!

He charmed Sonia's mum the way he had charmed me — I wondered if Sonia had ever taken him home last year. If she had, it didn't look as if her mum remembered it. I began to feel quite jealous that he was paying more attention to her than me!

Then he saw Sonia collecting her waterproof trousers and big boots.

'Can't we give you a lift?' he said.

You should have seen the look in John's eyes — as if he was ashamed that he had only a motorbike and Sonia's clothes and hair would be crushed. There was also fear that she might say yes.

She didn't.

'No, thank you.' She said this frostily, and John's smile broadened.

So did mine.

'Shall we go, then?' I said brightly. I didn't want to hang about waiting for John and Sonia to get into all their cumbersome clothes, and I was sure they didn't want me to either.

Clive took the hint, and we shouted goodbye to Sonia's mum and dad, keeping tactfully out of the way in their sitting room.

'There, you see,' Clive said to me as he opened the car door for me. 'I don't present too much of a problem to mothers, do I? I can be quite civilised.'

'It isn't that,' I began, but it would be too difficult to explain and I didn't want to spoil the evening. 'Perhaps next time Sonia can come to ours and . . .'

'The next school dance?' He was rather coldly amused, I thought, as if this was the last time he would ever get himself dragged into these childish games. 'How often do you have them? Once a term? Once a year?'

'Oh, well,' I said, fighting to keep my voice casual, 'by next year my wicked stepmother may have bitten the poisoned apple.'

'Or you'll have been carried off by a different prince,' he said.

I laughed with him, but I didn't want to think of it ending. Sonia's time with him was short enough – was it going to happen to me as well? For the hundredth time I wondered why . . . perhaps, now that Sonia and I were firm friends again, I would be able to ask her some time.

It's funny when you've been looking forward to something for a long time – for weeks all through exam time, for weeks since yesterday evening – suddenly there's something better. I just wanted to go on driving through the night with Clive. I didn't want to go anywhere, didn't want to have to speak to anyone else, to be sociable and dance. But then, I wouldn't be able to take him over to the buffet table and say casually, 'Oh, by the way, I made those,' and wait for his admiring comments.

If he did comment admiringly, of course. I was beginning to learn that Clive didn't always react the way I expected or wanted him to.

However, we were here, and I began to feel excited again. They'd be so envious, all of them, seeing me with this gorgeous bloke, seeing the way he treated me, so differently from those few I knew about, whose boyfriends sometimes seemed to pretend they weren't there because they were too embarrassed to acknowledge they were going out with them.

And then the first person I saw was Alan.

Chapter 10

After the shock, I told myself there was no reason why he shouldn't be there. Just because he was going out with a girl called Julie at college didn't mean to say that someone else in our year might not have asked him to the disco. I didn't have any rights over Alan. As he had always said, during those interminable conversations with my mother, he was free to talk to or be friends with whoever he liked, that no one had ownership over any other human being. I had agreed with them at the time, but at this moment I felt rather possessive towards Clive, and I know I'd probably have felt annoyed if he'd wanted to ask someone else out tonight.

There weren't very many people yet – we were too

early, I realised – so I couldn't melt into the crowd before he saw me, even if I wanted to. And of course, being Alan, he came over straight away to say hello.

I just wanted to curl up and die. I could almost feel the razor blades come out of Clive's eyes to cut off Alan's friendly words. I suppose it was because he sounded so relaxed with me, as if he'd known me all my life, which of course he had, so there was no need for Clive to go all possessive like that.

'Who's that?' he said sharply when Alan had gone off again with Angela. I knew her fairly well – a blonde, slim friend of Jane's from a different form. She lived over in Alan's end of town, which I suppose is how she knew him.

'Alan? Oh, he's an old friend of the family,' I said. I hoped it sounded light enough. 'We were brought up together. My mother and his were best friends.'

I went on telling him about our backgrounds – I just couldn't stop talking. It seemed as if I had to explain right down to the last detail that Alan wasn't a boyfriend of mine, though I didn't tell Clive about our parents' sneaking hopes, even though we always laughed about them.

The explanation seemed to satisfy him though, because he became the nice Clive again – attentive and loving. I was so proud to be with him. I had been right about him being the best-looking bloke. Everyone else's partners looked young and spotty and awkward, and there were a lot of people without partners at all – boys who hung around at the back of the hall and laughed loudly, and girls who giggled in groups, hoping someone would ask them to dance.

I could see what Clive meant about it not being

his scene. It wasn't at all really. I almost wished I hadn't been so determined that he should come. Then when we started dancing I stopped wishing it, and because he was so good and enjoyed showing it off he was a lot more cheerful. When at last we sat down, breathless, he said, 'The decoration's very good.'

It was, too. We had spent all Friday doing it. Since we'd finished exams they let us off lessons all day to get the hall ready. We'd hung swathes of paper flowers from the thick curtains, hundreds of them, so that when the disco lights flashed round, it was like sitting in a tropical garden instead of the old school hall. It was a tropical theme – we'd got great palms branching across the ceiling. Our English teacher, who was helping us hang them up, muttered dire things about fire regulations, but didn't object. I suppose if there'd been an accident the whole place would have gone up like dry tinder, but there wasn't, and it didn't.

And then the food.

Everybody had really gone to town making things. There were savoury pastries like mine (though I was glad to see nobody had done anything as good-looking as mine – thanks to Dad!), salads, gorgeous looking puds like Sonia's mother makes, cakes, gâteaux – you name it, we'd probably got it spread out on that length of table.

'Which is yours?' said Clive as I led him through as near the front as possible. It wasn't that I was feeling hungry, or being greedy. I just wanted him to see my efforts before the rest of the crowd got their hands on them.

'How do you know I've made anything?' I quipped.

'You must have,' he said. 'I've never been hustled so fast in my life!'

'Oh, sorry.'

'I don't mind,' he said. 'Am I allowed three, or is that being too greedy?'

'Have four,' I said. 'I did four different sorts. Here— ' and I took his plate and selected the best-looking of the little tartlets and pasties. 'These are mine. You can choose your own of the rest.'

'Gorgeous!' he said with his mouth full, pastry crumbs at the corner of his mouth, without even waiting to get to the salad. 'Now I know what heaven's like.'

'Frankie's cooking?' came Alan's mocking voice from behind us. 'It must have improved in the last fortnight, then.'

I gave him a look that should have murdered him.

'You're always too busy yakking to my mother,' I said sourly. 'Try these, if you want to know what my cooking's really like. But I should think you'd much rather try Angela's.'

'I didn't do anything,' admitted Angela. 'Can't cook for toffee.'

'There you are, then,' I said nastily. 'You won't be able to get poisoned. Do you want any of this salad, Clive?'

Why did I feel so nervy and jumpy when Alan came near Clive? There wasn't any need. I'd explained about our friendship, and Clive had seemed to understand. He wasn't looking razor-bladish now, just ordinarily sociable. But I didn't want to risk anything. I hurried him along the line of dishes until we had our plates piled full, then led him to one of the furthest corners of the hall underneath a bower of ivy, paper flowers and palm fronds.

'This is cosy,' said Clive. 'And I think your food is wonderful, truly, in spite of what your friend says.' There was heavy emphasis on 'your friend'.

'I've never made him anything as far as I remember,' I said. 'He wouldn't know.'

The atmosphere lightened perceptibly, and the hall darkened again as the DJ decided it was time he got back into gear again and that people should have had enough to eat.

'I'll take the plates back, shall I?' offered Clive.

'Please.'

I watched him sidestep the few people who had got up to begin another dance and admired the way he walked.

'My turn,' said a voice.

'Oh, Alan – you made me jump.' I grinned up at him. He wasn't a patch on Clive for looks, but he looked good all the same.

'Dance?' he said.

'Well – shouldn't I wait till Clive comes back?' I said.

'I'd have thought it would be better *not* to wait till Clive comes back. He might say no.'

'Don't be ridiculous,' I said. 'Of course he wouldn't say no. Because . . .'

'You wouldn't ask him,' finished Alan at the same time as me, and we laughed in our old, companionable way.

'Well, quite,' I said. 'I just thought it might be polite, that's all.'

'He'll be some time,' said Alan. 'There's a big

queue for drinks. You mean he doesn't mind caterers' orange?'

'He hasn't . . .' I began, but he might, of course, knowing Clive. It was the sort of nice thing he would do. In which case, he wouldn't mind at all if I had a dance with Alan instead of sitting glumly in the corner all by myself.

He pulled my arm and led me right into the thick of the dancers in the middle of the floor. It was a really fast number, with a fantastic beat and we whirled about the floor as if we were exhibition dancers.

When it ended I panted, 'I didn't know you could dance like that.'

'You never asked,' he said imperturbably. 'Am I as good as him?'

'Who? Clive? Oh, if you put your mind to it and practised every day you might get within ninety marks,' I said flippantly.

'I'll keep trying,' he said, and laid an arm ever so casually across my shoulders as we walked back to the corner.

I hadn't expected to see Clive back there. I suppose I'd believed Alan when he said he must have gone for drinks. He quite obviously hadn't. He was sitting, rather stiffly, his mouth in a hard line.

'You'd better go and rescue Angela,' I said, feeling my temper rise a little. Why should he go all grotty just because I had a dance with an old friend?

'Yes,' said Alan. 'She wanted ice cream and I didn't.'

I felt an absurd flattening of disappointment. So he hadn't asked me to dance because he really wanted to. It was just a convenient way of using up time while he waited for her to finish her ice cream. Any other time and I could have said so, with a viperish sting in my words, knowing that Alan would have taken it as a joke and milked the venom easily from my fangs.

Perhaps it was because I couldn't get rid of the poison in my heart, perhaps it was the sight of Clive's bad-tempered face when I couldn't see what he had to get bad-tempered about, that made me react the way I did.

'I thought you came to this dance with me,' said Clive tightly when I sat down beside him.

I could feel my smile freeze on my face.

It stayed smiling, but I couldn't move my mouth properly.

'I did,' I said. 'I thought you'd gone for drinks.'

Though I didn't see why I should have to explain anything at all.

'I was just taking our plates back. You knew I wouldn't be long.'

'Alan said you were probably queuing,' I said lightly, 'so I thought I'd have a quick fling before you got back.'

Of course, I would use the wrong word. You try to be honest with people, so that you don't get in a tangle, but when I'm honest with people I say it all wrong and get into a far worse tangle.

'A quick fling,' he said. 'Yes. I think I understand.'

'What do you mean, understand?' I said hotly. 'There's nothing at all to understand. If I can't have a dance with an old friend . . .'

'How many more "old friends" have you got here?'

He was a bit like a little boy, sulky and rude.

'Oh, Clive! Honestly, there's nothing like that at all. I told you about Alan – I've just known him for years, that's all. If I'd known it would upset you I wouldn't have danced with him at all. All right?'

'All right,' he said reluctantly. 'But just remember I'm here with you and don't dance with anyone else.'

I hadn't, up till that moment. I suppose it always happens – if somebody tells you not to do something, immediately you want to. I didn't really want to dance with anyone else at all anyway. Nobody else was so exciting to dance with. I think I convinced him. In any case, he got up for the next number, pulling me across so violently that it hurt, and threw himself into the fast beat as if punishing the floor.

But it didn't spoil his dancing at all. It was still fantastic. Perhaps anger made him more brilliant than ever, because after a while the other dancers moved away a little so that we were in the middle of the floor, doing an exhibition dance like we had at Jocasta's before his friends came along. The little storm of applause when we'd finished set him in a mad mood, and we spent the rest of the evening on the floor. He wouldn't let me stop for an instant.

Then it was the end. The lights flickered and went dimmer, and the DJ announced the last dance. Surprisingly, it was a proper waltz – a real old-fashioned record like I suppose my parents might have danced to when they were young. And I didn't know how to do it! I don't think Clive did either, but it didn't matter. He just held me tightly and close, his face against mine, giving me little tiny kisses as we shuffled on the floor, our feet just walking to the music.

I felt wonderful. Safe and secure in his arms. I didn't want this dance to end.

But it did end. The spell was broken. The lights began to glow brighter again, and I pulled Clive away to get our coats before they grew too bright and spoiled the illusions in there.

I snuggled against him in the chilly car.

'You were wonderful,' I murmured.

He turned and kissed me. I shivered again, but not with the cold.

'You were wonderful too,' he said. 'We make a fantastic team, don't we?'

He could have gone on talking to me like that all night. It was bliss, hearing him say all those things, hinting that we would be together for ever.

He drove slowly, but it was still too fast. We don't live far enough away from school.

'Stop before the corner,' I begged. It was darker there, and I thought, before I had to go, his arms would come round me and I could feel his warmth and those kisses which sent thrills of pleasure through me.

'No,' he said. 'I'm taking you right home.'

I sat up suddenly. Home. No. They'd be up still. It wasn't like Jocasta's, when they'd gone to bed.

'Don't be silly,' I said. 'There's a street light right outside our front gate. You don't want the neighbours nosying, do you?'

'No,' he said, and I didn't hear the tightness come into his voice until it was too late. 'I want to be able to take you to your door like an ordinary boyfriend would. What's the matter with you? Why can't I come to your house? The way your ex-boyfriend was talking it seems as if your parents are ordinary enough. He knows them, why can't I know them?'

I was dumb. I didn't know how to answer. I don't know why, but I still had this stupid feeling that I didn't want him to meet my mother. He wasn't her type. He just wouldn't understand her direct way of talking.

'I don't . . .' I began, but he didn't want to listen to me.

'In case your boyfriend is there, I suppose?' he said harshly. 'Is that why? Is he there all the time, or aren't you sure? Is that why? Just in case I bump into him by accident?'

'Don't be silly, Clive!' I cried. 'There isn't anything like that at all. I don't know what you're talking about.'

'No?' he sneered. 'What about having a dance with him as soon as my back is turned? You just couldn't wait, could you?'

I was furious by now, but instead of shouting at him – which I would have done at Alan if he'd talked to me like that – I burst into tears.

'There isn't anything like that!' I said through my sobs. 'Honestly, there isn't. I just had a dance with a friend, but I won't again if you don't like it.'

'You won't, that's for sure,' said Clive. 'Not if you come out with me again. All right, come and prove there's nothing between you two.'

I realised that we were still driving through the dark streets, but we weren't anywhere I knew.

'Where are we going?' I said, suddenly frightened.

He didn't answer. I could see the grim set of his mouth under the last of the street lamps.

Chapter 11

We were travelling down a tunnel of light where the road unrolled in front of us and branches swept the roof in short strokes. It was velvet dark when we stopped and he turned off the lights.

His kisses this time weren't gentle and thrilling. His mouth was hard, and I began to panic.

'Clive, I— '

He grabbed me tighter. My head was banging against the back of the seat and his fingers dug into my shoulders painfully. I kept moving my head, trying to get away from the brusing lips.

'*Clive*!'

He pushed me away from him roughly and I could feel his eyes glare at me.

'You said he didn't mean anything to you. All right, I'll believe you, but I forbid you to see him again.'

'But I can't refuse to see him, Clive,' I said helplessly. 'He's my friend. You can't suddenly say to friends, "Go away, I don't want to see you ever again." I like him. He's part of my life.'

How could I say it without making him more angry? He just wouldn't understand.

'Well, if you want to be part of my life you've got to stop seeing him.'

'Don't be silly, Clive,' I tried to reason. 'He's a family friend. He'd come round to see my mother even if he didn't come to see me.'

'Yes, this mother of yours,' he interrupted. 'If *he's* good enough for your mother, why aren't I? What's so funny about me that I'm not allowed in your home?'

I didn't even think of the obvious retort that he hadn't asked me to his home. Not just then. Why can't I ever think of the right thing to say at the right moment? I said the wrong thing again. Trying to make things better, I just made things worse.

'You wouldn't have got on,' I said. 'You wouldn't like her.'

It was only a little bit of the truth, and the way I said it, I suppose it did sound a bit funny.

'So I'm not good enough for your family?' he sneered. 'Who are you, Miss Bighead, to say who's suitable for me?'

'But if you think that, why don't you want me to go on seeing Alan?' I said, stung to retort.

'If you can't see that . . .'

As if I was too exasperating for words, he stopped in mid-sentence and grabbed me tightly again, pulling my face to his for another of those hurtful, bruising kisses. I gasped for breath and tried to push him away again, but it only made him hold tighter.

I really began to feel scared now. All these warnings you get from teachers and television and – even with her liberal ideas – my mother, I thought I was in for instant rape. I had to get away from him. He didn't know what he was doing. He was too angry to reason with. All these and other muddled thoughts kept going round my head as I tried to keep my face away from his.

I had one arm free. If I could find the handle . . .

I'd found it. I hoped it was for the door and not the window.

But I didn't have any idea where we were. I'd have to run along the country roads in my high heels, without a coat, in my cotton dress. And he would be able to catch me before I'd run a couple of yards . . .

I sobbed under the insistent mouth. I didn't know what to do.

And then, as I thought at least I could try, and had begun to pull at the door handle, I saw lights come up behind us. Another car. Don't go away. Wait till I . . .

Clive moved for an instant, and I took my chance.

I yanked at the car door and caught him off balance, pushing him against the steering wheel in my urge to get out. I had to wave at this car before it drove past, leaving me to what nameless fate I didn't want to try to imagine.

My legs were out, I pulled desperately away from Clive's clinging arm.

If he hadn't let me go I'd have screamed and dragged myself away to run right into the middle of the road in front of the oncoming car.

But it stopped.

I stumbled into the lights, sobbing and waving my arms.

'Hey, hang on – I might have run you over.'

The voice was achingly, wonderfully familiar.

'Alan – I—'

I was too out of breath to explain. I didn't want to explain. I was ashamed.

'Need any help?' he said.

I stopped panicking. I had been stupid. If I'd just said to Clive I didn't want him grabbing me like that he would have stopped. I felt a sudden loyalty to him.

'The car's broken down,' I said loudly. Clive would hear, through the opened door.

I heard him open the door on his side and step out into the lights.

'Can I do anything?' Alan's voice was ordinarily friendly. My heart stopped pounding and I felt safe.

Clive's voice was equally ordinary – or was it elaborately casual?

'Not much wrong,' he said. 'I can deal with it in a couple of minutes.'

'That's all right, then,' said Alan, still friendly. But I knew him well. That tone said oceans to me. 'Do you need a torch?'

He was going to keep Clive talking, make sure the car was working, before he would let me go.

'That would help,' said Clive sulkily. 'Difficult,' he laughed, 'to do things by feel.'

'I didn't know you had a car,' I said. It was as much to see if my own voice had stopped shaking as to ask for information.

'It's Dad's. I borrowed it to take Angela home. She lives quite a way out, a mile further down this road. No buses this time of night. And it was better than her family having to turn out for her.'

'I didn't even know you could drive,' I said helplessly.

'Ages ago,' he said cheerfully. 'Not long after my seventeenth birthday.'

You see, Clive, I said silently. I didn't even know about that. Of course I wasn't two-timing you. I hoped he had heard, and got the message.

'Shall I take Frankie back, then, if you've got to

do things to the car? It's a bit cold, and her parents might worry.'

'It's all right,' I said. 'You could phone them, couldn't you? Or drop by on your way home?' I didn't know where we were, whether this was reasonable.

'It's not on my way home,' said Alan. 'But I don't mind taking you back. You don't know how long this — breakdown — will take to be mended.'

'It's nothing serious,' said Clive. I could hear the hardness in his tone. He was furious, I knew, at Alan's high-handed attitude. 'It'll only take about ten minutes to fix.'

'I'm sure it will,' said Alan drily. 'Come on, Frankie.'

He took hold of my arm, none too gently. Suddenly I was absolutely furious myself. I was getting fed up with these blokes thinking they could tell me what to do.

'I'll stay with Clive,' I said stiffly.

'No,' said Clive. 'You'd better do as he says. I don't really know how long this will take. I think you'd be wiser.'

'Thank you very much,' I said in a cold fury. 'Well, Clive, it's been a nice evening. Thank you for coming with me.'

I'd show him I could behave well when the situation demanded.

I could see the wry twist of his mouth in Alan's headlights.

'Don't mention it,' he said. 'I enjoyed myself.'

And so with these stiffly polite words we parted. He said nothing about phoning me. At the time I didn't care. I sat in the passenger seat of Alan's father's car, rigid as a piece of wood, and about as communicative.

Outside our house he parked, then turned to speak to me. His face looked worried in the street light. I don't remember ever seeing Alan look anything but self-possessed before.

'Would you rather I'd left you?' he said. 'I'm sorry. It was because you jumped out at me like that. I thought . . .'

'Perfectly all right,' I said icily.

'You were frightened, weren't you? Come on, Frankie, I've known you long enough.'

'That's why,' I said.

'Why what?'

'He was jealous. Because you danced with me. Because I've known you so long.'

'I know,' he said. 'I knew about Sonia, too. She couldn't stand being possessed, either.'

'Sonia!' My best friend. Both my best friends. And they kept it quiet, the pair of them. I was indignant. I said so.

'You wouldn't have listened,' said Alan.

'No,' I said. 'I suppose I wouldn't. Anyway, who are you to judge who I go out with?'

'I didn't,' he said. 'But knowing you − I didn't think you'd be happy with someone like that. I didn't think . . . oh, never mind.'

He sounded strained. He began to open his door.

'I hope I haven't spoiled everything,' he said.

'I expect you have,' I said. 'But it was a bit spoiled anyway. It's not really your fault. Not really.' In fact, not at all, I decided. 'Oh, shut up, Alan. I've had enough of this. I'm going in.'

I opened the car door and marched up our front path. I could hear him lock the doors and follow me. I didn't wait for him at our front door, just left it open while I went straight upstairs to take off my shoes and put on a jumper over the green dress.

'Alan! How nice. You're quite a stranger these days.'

Of course, she *would* make a fuss of him, I thought sourly. Here we go again, all the arguments and discussions that I'm supposed to take part in too.

Sulkily, I went downstairs. It was all very well staying up there, but there isn't much point in being a martyred heroine if nobody takes any notice of you. I might as well be sulky in front of them, then perhaps they might feel interested in me instead of him.

I didn't want to go straight into the sitting room, so I put on a kettle and laid out mugs and a teapot on the big tray. By the time the tea was ready and I took it through they were well into a discussion about something or other.

'Frankie, we've been talking . . .'

And there I was again, drawn into it, having to give my opinion, having to give my reasons.

It was oddly comfortable.

Later, when I took the pot round for second cups, they remembered I'd been out.

'What was the hop like, Frankie?' asked my father. 'What did they think of my cooking?'

'I knew it wouldn't have been Frankie's,' said Alan. 'But the fellow she was with liked them. Great compliments.'

'Good,' said Dad. 'But she did make them, you know. I just stood on the sidelines and shouted "foul" when she did something wrong.'

No comment on the 'fellow she was with'. I felt grateful. I didn't want to have to explain about Clive. It had been enough of an evening having to explain *to* him.

'Must be all right if he liked Frankie's cooking,' said my mother. She was sitting on the floor against Dad's knees, keeping the fire off everyone else. I often wished she wouldn't do this; it seemed so, well, I suppose undignified in a mother. But tonight I had an enormous affection for her. For both of them. And Alan.

'I don't know whether I liked him all that much,' I said bravely, looking straight at Alan. 'He seemed to think I couldn't say hello to any of my friends when I was with him.'

'No?' said Alan, looking directly at me. We never had to say much. We knew each other so well.

And then they got into a long discussion about the freedom of the individual and whether you had the right to tell somebody you couldn't be friends with someone else. Of course this led to nationalism and politics of all kinds.

I began to feel sleepy. I just let them go on talking. It was homely and familiar, and I really didn't want it any other way. I tried to imagine Clive coping with their ideas. He just wouldn't agree. I couldn't really see him arguing the way they do anyway. He'd get all upset if you disagreed with him.

The next person I went out with, I decided, would just have to put up with my mother. He'd also have to put up with me seeing a lot of Alan. That was a friendship I really couldn't throw away in a hurry.

I woke up all of a sudden. My parents were saying goodnight, Mum taking the tray and Dad gathering up stray cups from the corners of the room. Alan was still sitting quite comfortably by the fire, gazing into the glowing depths, not in a hurry to move at all.

I cleared my throat. There was suddenly something very urgent I wanted to know.

'Your — Julie — is she — nice?'

'Very nice,' said Alan, still staring into the flickering flame which licked a corner of coal.

'That's good.'

It wasn't good at all. I don't know whether I'd have realised about Alan if Clive hadn't been all jealous, but I knew quite definitely that Alan's friendship was something I didn't ever want to lose. And if this Julie didn't want Alan to be friends with me . . .

'Does she mind — you coming here?' I said in a small voice.

'No. Why should she?'

'Because — oh, I don't know.'

I didn't know how to explain, or ask. I was just terrified that just as I had got to realise how very dear Alan was to me, I might lose him completely to someone who felt like Clive about relationships.

'I wouldn't go out with anyone who tried to own me, you know that,' he said.

'No. I suppose you wouldn't.'

He was much more honest with himself than I was. I was prepared, for a while, to reject Alan because

Clive told me to. It was something Alan could be trusted never to do.

'I wasn't staying away because of Julie, you know,' he said. 'Only I thought you wanted the field clear.'

'Mum missed you,' I said.

'*I* missed *you*,' he said.

'But – Julie— ' I began stupidly.

'Julie and I have been friends for a long time. I've known Angela even longer. I know lots of people, male and female, as you very well know. But hadn't you realised you're the only girl I ever wanted? To be with for ever, I mean?'

My heart began to pound. No, I hadn't realised that at all. What I *had* realised, though, was that Alan was the only person I ever wanted to be with. For ever.

'We know each other very well, Frankie,' he said softly.

He had moved over from his side of the fireplace to the chair I was sitting on.

'Shift up,' he said.

There was room for the two of us – squeezed together tight. His arm round my shoulders hadn't the same thrill as Clive's arm had, but it felt as if it belonged there. I let my head rest against his shoulder and sighed.

'I really hate to let my mother be right again,' I said.

'What about?' said Alan.

'What she and your mother have gone on about for years.'

'Oh, that,' said Alan. 'Awful, to admit they're right, isn't it? But this time we've got to let them have their way.'

He bent forward and kissed me full on the mouth.

This time the thrill was more than Clive's touch had ever given me. There was a feeling of – rightness about it.

I let my arms come up and hold him as we shifted more comfortably in the big chair.

Whatever happened – whoever we were friends with – there was something special about Alan and me. We were friends – for keeps!

	ven	Laura Black	£1.75p
		Freda Bright	£1.50p
		Jackie Collins	£2.50p
☐		Robin Cook	£1.95p
☐	**The Entity**	Frank De Felitta	£2.50p
☐	**The Dead of Jericho**	Colin Dexter	£1.50p
☐	**Whip Hand**	Dick Francis	£1.75p
☐	**Saigon**	Anthony Grey	£2.95p
☐	**The White Paper Fan**	Unity Hall	£1.95p
☐	**Solo**	Jack Higgins	£1.95p
☐	**The Rich are Different**	Susan Howatch	£3.50p
☐	**Smash**	Garson Kanin	£1.75p
☐	**Smiley's People**	John le Carré	£2.50p
☐	**The Conduct of Major Maxim**	Gavin Lyall	£1.75p
☐	**The Master Mariner Book 1: Running Proud**	Nicholas Monsarrat	£1.50p
☐	**Fools Die**	Mario Puzo	£2.50p
☐	**The Throwback**	Tom Sharpe	£1.95p
☐	**Wild Justice**	Wilbur Smith	£2.50p
☐	**Cannery Row**	John Steinbeck	£1.95p
☐	**Caldo Largo**	Earl Thompson	£1.95p
☐	**Ben Retallick**	E. V. Thompson	£2.50p

All these books are available at your local bookshop or newsagent, or can be ordered direct from the publisher. Indicate the number of copies required and fill in the form below   12

....

Name_____
(Block letters please)

Address_____

_____

Send to CS Department, Pan Books Ltd, PO Box 40, Basingstoke, Hants
Please enclose remittance to the value of the cover price plus:
35p for the first book plus 15p per copy for each additional book ordered
to a maximum charge of £1.25 to cover postage and packing
Applicable only in the UK

While every effort is made to keep prices low, it is sometimes
necessary to increase prices at short notice. Pan Books reserve
the right to show on covers and charge new retail prices which
may differ from those advertised in the text or elsewhere